TILL DEATH DO US PART

STEPHEN TAYLOR

COVER DESIGN BY
DISSECT DESIGNS
WWW.DISSECTDESIGNS.COM

www.dissectdesigns.com

Copyright © 2024 Stephen Taylor
All rights reserved.

ISBN: 9798340112248

DANNY PEARSON WILL RETURN

For updates about current and upcoming releases, as well as exclusive promotions, visit the authors website at:

www.stephentaylorbooks.com

ALSO BY STEPHEN TAYLOR
THE DANNY PEARSON THRILLER SERIES

Snipe

Heavy Traffic

The Timekeepers Box

The Book Signing

Vodka Over London Ice

Execution of Faith

Who Holds The Power

Alive Until I Die

Sport of Kings

Blood Runs Deep

Command to Kill

No Upper Limit

Leave Nothing To Chance

Won't Stay dead

Till Death Do Us Part

Enemy At The Door

CHAPTER 1

'Keep your guard up and watch for the opening. He's got a habit of leaving his ribs open on the left,' Big Dave shouted across from the punch bag he was holding for one of the lads working on his combination punches.

'Oof, thanks Dave,' Danny said, moving around the boxing ring after Nikki side-stepped and drove a knee into his exposed ribs.

'Don't leave yourself open and you won't get hit, will you, soft lad,' Dave shouted over his shoulder.

'Yeah, soft lad, don't leave yourself open,' Nikki teased, her hands up protecting her face while she kept her elbows loose, ready to whip across or open up to throw a punch.

'I'll let you have that one. Now, let's see if you can get me again,' Danny said, grinning as he adjusted his stance and raised his gloves.

At her request, and after all the things that had happened to them since they'd met, Danny had been teaching Nikki how to defend herself using his boxing experience and the Krav Maga mixed martial arts form of fighting he'd learned in the SAS. They'd only been at it for three months, but he had to admit she was getting pretty good. Danny pulled his punches a little, holding back on his power and aggression as they exchanged blows. He allowed Nikki to see his moves coming and react the way he'd taught her to. As they danced around the ring, he sensed someone moving between the punch bags hung around the backroom of Dave Pullman's Gym, used as a boxing and mixed martial arts training room. The figure moved up to the side of the boxing ring behind him. Danny instinctively turned his head to see who it was. Seeing the opening, Nikki darted forward, aiming to plant a left hook to Danny's jaw. Reacting on instinct at her incoming fist, Danny flicked his elbow up, blocking the punch while sweeping her legs away with a spinning kick. Nikki landed flat on her back with a boom on the padded canvas floor.

'Shit, sorry, you ok?' Danny said, offering his hand to pull her up.

'Yeah, you'll have to do better than that to keep me down,' she said, smiling as she took his hand and he pulled her up.

'Oh wow, it takes a big man to put a wee girly on the floor,' came a thick Scottish accented voice from behind.

Danny turned and Nikki looked around him at the man standing at the side of the ring.

'So you think you could do better then?' Nikki said defensively.

'As a matter of fact I do,' he said, slipping his jacket off and ducking under the ropes into the ring.

Danny's eyes narrowed and the muscles in his cheeks

flexed as he ground his teeth together. He backed up as Nikki climbed out of the ring and the guy stepped in.

'Ok, Twinkle Toes, let's go, round one, ding, ding,' the man said. He was a little shorter than Danny, with a stocky, solid build.

The two of them took up an almost identical stance, legs bent, hands up and loose, guarding the head with their elbows raised, forming a triangle that enabled them to defend and attack from. Both men engaged in a brief explosion of blows and blocks before backing away and circling each other. The second time they moved in, the man blocked Danny as he drove a knee into his ribs. He darted a punch over the top of Danny's arms, catching him just above the temple, his knuckles skidding off the side of Danny's head before they backed away again. As the guy grinned, Danny's face darkened. They went in again. This time, Danny attacked at ferocious speed, ducking the guy's punches to deliver a fast combination of blows to his stomach. Danny grabbed one of the guy's arms and spun his back to him, throwing the man over his shoulder to smack him down on the canvas with a loud boom. In a split second, Danny dropped onto the canvas behind him and threw his arm around the man's neck, locking him in a tight choke hold.

'Ok, ok,' he blurted out in a whispered gasp.

Danny released him and jumped to his feet, staring down at him for a second or two before his face softened and broke into a grin.

'How are you doing, Ferg? You always were better at shooting things than hand-to-hand combat,' Danny said, offering his old SAS buddy a hand.

'Yeah, well, next time I'll just shove the barrel of a gun

up your arse and pull the trigger,' Fergus McKinsey said, taking his hand and grinning back.

'Nice to see you, Fergus,' Nikki said from outside the ring.

'You too, Nikki darlin'. Are you sure you want to marry this big oaf? It's not too late to bin him off and run away with a red-blooded Scotsman.'

'Attractive as that offer sounds, I think I'll stick with the oaf,' Nikki said, chuckling.

'I am here you know,' Danny said, walking up to the ropes to hold them apart for Fergus to climb out.

'Alright touchy, Jesus, you're getting really sensitive in your old age,' Fergus said, jumping down from the ring and rolling his shoulder around. 'I think you broke my drinking arm.'

'As long as it's not the one you get your wallet out with, we'll be ok,' Danny said, chuckling.

'What? Wallet? I thought this little shindig was on the posh twat soon to be your brother-in-law, Scott?' Fergus said, before quickly adding, 'No offence, love,' to Nikki, remembering Scott was her brother.

'None taken,' Nikki replied, always enjoying the banter when Danny and his old SAS mates got together.

'Ferg, behave yourself. He's my best friend and Nikki's brother, and it's good of Scott to stump up for the flights and hotel. The least you can do is put your hand in your pocket for drinks,' Danny said, frowning at Fergus.

'Ok, ok, keep your hair on. So when are Charles and my good friend Scott joining us?' Fergus said, putting on a posh accent.

'They'll be at our house for one, the taxi to the airport's booked for two,' said Danny, unable to stop himself from smiling at Fergus's comment.

4

'Great, but if Scott calls me a caveman again, I'm gonna throw him out of the plane mid-flight,' Fergus said, following Danny and Nikki out of the gym, shaking his head.

'Don't worry, get a few drinks into him and Scott and they'll be fine,' Danny said to Nikki.

They went back to Danny's house and spent the time chatting and catching up until Chaz arrived, closely followed by Scott.

'Alright, Chaz,' Danny said, answering the door.

'Alright and raring to go, mate. Make the most of this, Danny boy. Once you're married, the only pleasure you'll have is taking a shit while she's out, so she doesn't make you clean the whole fucking bathroom afterwards.'

'Go on through. Ferg's in the kitchen,' Danny said, shaking his head.

'Afternoon, Daniel, are we all ready for the off?' said Scott, dressed in a beige Ralph Lauren linen suit while wheeling a large Emporio Armani suitcase.

'You do know we're off to Benidorm, not Saint-Tropez?'

'Just because we're off to Blackpool in the sun, that's no reason to let one's standards slip.'

'Ok, whatever makes you happy, Scotty boy,' Danny said, listening to raised voices and cheering coming from the kitchen.

'Come on, guys, for fuck's sake we haven't even got to the airport yet,' Danny yelled, entering the kitchen to see Chaz and Fergus downing their second beer in two minutes.

After calming down and having a few slower beers, the taxi arrived to take them to the airport.

'Ok, time for the off. Wish me luck,' Danny said with a grin to Nikki.

5

'You're going to need it. Look, just have fun. It's a shame your brother can't go, but with Tina about to pop at any minute.'

'I know, it can't be helped. Let me know if the baby decides to put in an appearance.'

'I will. Enjoy yourself, I'll see you when you get back,' Nikki said, popping up on tiptoes to kiss him.

'Put her down for Christ's sake, we're losing drinking time here,' shouted Chaz from the taxi.

Danny and Nikki parted. He grinned and gave her a wink before walking slowly to the taxi.

CHAPTER 2

'Are you sure you don't want me to call for a limousine to take us to the hotel?' Scott said, frowning, while trying not to touch anything as he stepped up onto an old battered transfer bus outside of Alicante airport.

There was a small scream and a woman's hand grabbed Chaz's arm to stop herself from falling to the ground when she tripped up the kerb. Chaz's reflexes were as fast as ever. He spun around and grabbed her around the waist, scooping her back up onto her feet.

'Oh, sorry about that. I was lucky there was a big strong man around to save me,' she said with a cheeky grin.

'You're welcome, love. Oi, hang on, lads, ladies first,' Chaz said, pushing Danny and Fergus aside to make room.

Scott stepped down off the bus, joining Danny and Fergus as they looked at Chaz grinning like a Cheshire cat while gesturing for two attractive women to step onto the bus ahead of them.

'There you go. I'm Chaz by the way,' he said, darting onto the bus behind them.

'Thanks Chaz, I'm Sandra and this is my sister Louise,' Sandra said with a smile and a little giggle.

Her sister Louise just gave him a nervous smile before sliding into a window seat to look out at the other buses in the car park.

'She alright?' Chaz said, nodding at Louise while Fergus slid into the window seat, allowing Chaz to sit in the seat on the opposite side of the aisle to Sandra.

'Yeah, she's ok. She just broke up with her fella. I can't really say much, but he was a right bastard, into all sorts of dodgy stuff. What about you?'

'You see this broken old married man sitting next to me and the even older guy in front who looks like he's had a really hard life?'

'Yeah, but I wouldn't call them old,' Sandra said, chuckling.

'Oh, trust me, they're old. Anyway, we were in the armed forces together and he's getting married, so we're here on his stag weekend,' Chaz said, pointing at Danny.

'What about the other one? The guy in the expensive suit, he looks kinda cute.'

'What can I say? Isn't it always the way? The gays are always good looking with great dress sense,' Chaz grinned.

'Oh, what a shame. Where are you staying?' Sandra said with a smile.

'Sandra!' her sister Louise said, looking apprehensive.

'What? There's no reason we can't have a little fun while we're out here,' Sandra turned and whispered back.

'I dunno, hang on. Oi, Scott, where are we staying?'

8

'A rather nice little five-star hotel, the Villa Venecia,' Scott said.

'Oh my god, that's where we're staying,' Sandra said excitedly.

'Great, perhaps you and your sister could join us for a drink?'

'Give me your number and I'll call you. It depends on how Louise is feeling,' Sandra said, looking towards her sister.

'Yeah, of course, no pressure, just if you fancy it,' Chaz said, doing a poor job of trying to look like he wasn't bothered, while putting his number into her phone.

'Here, store this and I'll call you later,' she said, calling him straight back, so he had her number in the call log.

They got dropped off at the Villa Venecia Hotel at around half past seven and waited patiently behind Sandra and Louise as they checked in and booked a massage, nails, and champagne on Louise's credit card.

'Perhaps we'll see you later,' Sandra said over her shoulder to Chaz as they headed off to their room, wheeling their bright pink suitcases along behind them.

'Er, what? Yes, that would be great.'

Danny, Fergus and Scott stood behind Chaz, chuckling as Sandra and Louise disappeared into the lift.

'Smooth, Chaz. How many years is it since you chatted someone up?' said Ferg, with a big grin on his face.

'That would be great. Jesus, what kind of response was that?' Chaz said, shaking his head.

'Yeah, with that and the state of your face, you've got no hope, mate,' Danny chipped in.

'What do you mean? I'm a catch. Look at me, I'm bloody gorgeous,' Chaz said, beaming.

'If you say so, Romeo. Come on, let's get checked in, we're losing drinking time,' Danny said.

'Her sister was a little strange though, scared of her own shadow,' Chaz said, more to himself than anyone else.

'Or scared of two old men and our good looking gay friend Scott,' Danny said, mocking Chaz for his comments on the bus.

'Er, yeah, well, alright, you're only a couple of years older than me, but Scott could still be gay.'

'Unbelievable, and to think you lot were Britain's elite fighting force,' said Scott, rolling his eyes as he handed out the room key cards.

The three of them just grinned at Scott before turning away from the lift to take the stairs up to the third floor.

'Ok, dump your stuff and meet down here in fifteen minutes. We've got some serious celebrating to do,' said Danny, lifting his carry-on bag to take the stairs two at a time. Fergus and Chaz followed close behind him, pulling each other back in a race to the top.

'This is going to be a very long weekend,' muttered Scott, pressing the button for the lift and stepping inside.

CHAPTER 3

'**D**ouglas, there's some people over at the rented house across the street, the one that woman's just moved into, er, what was her name?'

'Sandra. They'll leave when they realise she's not there. What kind of people?' Douglas shouted from his study.

'Big, mean-looking people. Douglas, they're not leaving, they've gone into her house,' Douglas's wife shouted back, her voice going up a pitch.

'What? Goddamned woman's hysterical,' Douglas muttered to himself as he slapped his Financial Times on the table and walked through to the lounge.

'Should I call the police?'

'Hold fire, my dear, I'm sure there's a perfectly innocent explanation. I'll go across and find out what's going on.'

Douglas exited the house and marched across the road towards Sandra's front door. It opened as he approached and a short, stocky, middle-aged man in a cheap, creased, black suit stepped forward, blocking his way.

'Can I help you, sir?'

'Yes, may I ask what you are doing here?' Douglas said, the retired sergeant major making it sound more like an order than a request.

'DCI Cain. Police business, sir. Now, if you wouldn't mind returning to your property,' Cain said, flashing his warrant badge at Douglas.

'Mmm, I see. Can you tell me what you want with Sandra?'

'We are just trying to ascertain the whereabouts of Miss Benning and her sister Louise Benning. We believe they may have witnessed a crime being committed and could have information that could help us. Nothing serious, just routine enquiries. You wouldn't happen to know where either of these women are, would you, sir?'

'I know she's gone away, but I don't know where.'

Just as Douglas finished speaking, a gust of wind blew the front door fully open to expose two men ransacking Sandra's living room, turning furniture over and slicing the sofa open with a knife.

'You're not police. Who the hell are—'

Douglas didn't get to finish his sentence. Cain stepped forward and punched a knife between Douglas's ribs to puncture his heart. He stayed on his feet for a few seconds, a look of shock and fear locked on his face until he dropped to a heap on the floor. As he went down, Douglas's wife appeared in Cain's eyeline as she watched from the lounge window in the house opposite.

'Alex,' Cain shouted to one of the men inside the house.

'Yes gov.'

'Go and take care of her. Keep it discreet,' he said, pointing to the house opposite.

'Yes gov,' Alex said, walking across the road at a fast

pace while Douglas's wife stood frozen to the spot, fear and panic taking away any rational thought of getting out of there.

From across the road, Cain watched as Alex appeared behind her to put one hand over her mouth and an arm around her neck, dragging her off out of sight.

'Anything?' he shouted to the other man in the lounge.

'No gov, it's not here.'

'Ok, put him in the boot and then drive across the road and pick up the wife and Alex,' Cain said, walking into the house as the other guy followed his orders.

He wandered around the kitchen, sifting through bits of paper and mail with his latex gloved hands, looking for any clue as to where Sandra and Louise Benning had gone, but found none.

His phone rang as he exited the property, pulling the front door shut behind him.

'DCI Cain,' he answered abruptly.

'Matt, it's Roger. You asked me to call you if we got any activity.'

'Go on, Roger.'

'She's in Spain. She used her credit card an hour ago at the Villa Venecia Hotel in Benidorm.'

'Good man, let me know if she uses it again,' Cain said, moving his thumb to kill the call.

'Wait, Matt.'

'What?'

'Look, this is dangerous. If I get found out, I'll lose my job and pension, er ...' There was a nervous pause before he continued. 'Tell the man I need more money.'

Cain rolled his eyes, unsurprised at the request from a whining prick with a gambling habit.

'Are you sure you want me to do that, Roger? You've

got a good thing going here. Do you really want to risk spoiling it?'

'I need more money. Tell him police Internal Affairs have been poking around the control centre investigating misconduct allegations. I'm taking a big risk for you. If I go down, we all go down,' Roger said, his voice growing in confidence as he spoke.

'Ok, calm down, Roger, I'll talk to him,' Cain said calmly.

'Thanks Matt.'

Cain hung up on him and looked up and down the road, shielding his eyes from the dipping summer sun. There was no one in sight so he crossed and climbed into the passenger seat of the BMW X5.

'Let's go. We'll get rid of these two at the farm on the way.'

'Yes gov,' Alex said, pulling away.

Cain sat looking at his phone for a minute or two, then called the number.

'Have you got it?' came a gruff response.

'No, there was nothing at the sister's house. But I know where she is.'

'Where?' the voice demanded, Cain barely having time to finish his sentence.

'The Villa Venecia Hotel, Benidorm.'

'Spain! Good work. I'll get Samuel Mendez to pick her up.'

'Mr Delany, there's something else,' Cain said, not sure how his next question would go down.

'What?'

'My guy, the one who got the address, he wants more money. He's worried about Internal Affairs finding out

14

about the information he's given us. He says if he goes down, we all do.'

The line went silent for a while. Cain knew better than to speak, so he just waited for his orders.

'He's become a liability. Take care of him.'

'Yes sir,' Cain replied without emotion.

'And Cain?'

'Yes sir,'

'Make it look like an accident.'

'Yes sir,' Cain replied, but Mr Delany had already hung up.

CHAPTER 4

Danny dumped his stuff and text Nikki to say he'd arrived safely and that he loved her, then headed out the door and along the hotel corridor towards the stairs. Halfway along, a door opened and Louise Benning stepped out into Danny's path. She let out a shriek as they bumped into each other, then backed away, clutching her bag with a terrified look on her face.

'Whoa, it's ok. No harm done. Are you OK?' Danny said, standing back and giving her a disarming smile.

'Sorry, it's ok. I'm sorry,' she said, turning quickly to tap the hotel card on the door and dart back inside with a scared look in her eyes.

Letting her go, Danny continued downstairs to the lobby to be greeted by cheers of 'Here comes the stag,' from Chaz and Fergus with a reserved smile from Scott.

'Come on then, where's the nearest bar?' Danny said, turning to Chaz as they exited the hotel. 'Hey Chaz, I just bumped into the sister of that woman you were chatting up on the bus. What's her story? She looked terrified,' Danny said quietly.

'Firstly, I wasn't chatting her up.'

'Yeah right,' Fergus chipped in.

'Er, her sister's just split up with some scumbag piece of shit boyfriend. She had to do a runner to get away from him. That's why they're here, so Louise can find an apartment to rent and start again.'

'Mm, that explains why she looked so scared when she ran into me,' Danny said, frowning.

'It was that, or the smell your aftershave's putting out. I'm leaning more towards the aftershave,' Fergus replied with a big grin.

'How any of you manage to attract anyone of the fairer sex is beyond me,' Scott said, looking the odd one out in his expensive suit against Danny, Chaz and Fergus in T-shirts, shorts and trainers.

'Pure animal attraction, Scotty boy,' Danny said, his frown dropping as he shook it off and got in the partying mood.

'I googled a nice little wine bar not far from here, if anyone's interested,' Scott piped up from the back.

'Is he joking?' Chaz said, turning to give Scott a look.

'No, I'm afraid he's not,' Danny said, laughing.

'It was only a suggestion. I'm happy to go and drink beer and sing football songs until we pass out along with all the other cavemen,' Scott muttered back with a slightly hurt look on his face.

'Come on, mate, no football songs or passing out, I promise,' Danny said, smiling at his friend.

They spent a few hours drinking their way around several bars, with only the briefest outbursts of football songs when another stag party piped up in a sports bar. With the rest of the weekend to go, and much to Fergus's dismay, they headed back towards the hotel, stopping at a bar just down the road from the hotel for one last drink.

'Come on, you lightweights, it's still early. We could go to that strip club near the town centre.'

'Behave,' said Danny.

'Perish the thought,' Scott tutted.

'Yeah, your Gaynor would love that one,' said Chaz as they all leaned across the table to slap Fergus on the back of the head.

'Alright, leave it out,' Fergus said, taking it in good humour as Chaz's phone rang.

'Sandra,' Chaz answered, unable to stop the grin spreading across his face.

'Do you still fancy that drink?'

'Yeah, of course.'

'Good, where are you?'

'We're in a little bar just down from the hotel. Come out the main entrance and turn left, you'll see us sitting outside,' Chaz said as the others all looked at him.

'Ok, we'll see you in a few minutes,' Sandra said, hanging up.

Danny and the others all cheered and slapped Chaz on the back.

'Well, fella, you've pulled. Get the drinks in, Chaz,' laughed Fergus.

A few minutes and a round of drinks later, Fergus spotted the two sisters walking down from the hotel on the dimly lit road.

'Here comes your girlfriend, Chaz.'

'She's not my bloody girlfriend, alright,' Chaz protested.

Danny wasn't listening. Two shadowy figures caught his attention as they appeared from around a corner a few metres behind the two women. The hairs on the back of his neck stood up. It was too dark to make them out clearly, but they moved with purpose, their heads up, eyes focused on the women. One of them held a phone to his ear as they quickened their pace to close the gap between them. Lights and vehicle noise made Danny turn his head. A Transit van turned into the road from the opposite direction and headed towards the women.

'Lads,' Danny said, getting up and starting to move.

His old SAS comrades instantly picked up on his body language, knowing the look as Danny's face hardened, watching as his eyes followed the van down the road. They were up in a flash, following Danny out of the bar to leave Scott with a white wine in his hand, wondering what was going on.

The van pulled up alongside the women, its side door opening before it came to a complete halt. Having caught up, the two men following the sisters grabbed them from behind. Sandra let out a shriek as the men pushed them towards their accomplice waiting inside the van. Danny spun around from the rear of the vehicle, his fist whistling past the side of Sandra's head to make contact with her assailant's cheek bone. As his head whipped back and hands let go of her, Chaz appeared from behind the van and shoved the edge of the open side door with all his might. It made a loud swishing noise as it hurtled towards closing on its runners, coming to a halt when it hit the man leaning out to grab the women, cracking his ribs as it sandwiched him between the edge of the door and the frame.

Fergus ran around the front of the van and came up behind the man pushing Louise. He cupped his hands and smacked them over the guy's ears as hard as he could. The man dropped to the floor like a lead balloon, losing his balance as both eardrums burst, leaving him concussed and in excruciating pain. Seeing this happen, the driver shouted something in Spanish as he revved up the van. The guy Danny had hit turned away from Sandra and pulled the passenger door open, barely getting in before the driver screamed away with the injured man in the back still hanging half in and half out of the vehicle.

'Are you ladies alright? You've got to be careful around these back streets at night,' Danny said, smiling to comfort the two shaking women.

'Thank you so much. What do you think they wanted?' Sandra said after a few moments.

'I don't know. Money, passports, they may have driven you to a cash point and made you withdraw as much as you could get. I'd ask this one, but I doubt he'd hear me.'

'You liked that, yeah? I've always wanted to try the old double ear slap. Bloody works a treat,' Fergus said, giving the man writhing on the floor a swift kick in the stomach for good measure.

'I suppose we'd better call the police. Scott speaks Spanish, doesn't he?' said Chaz.

'No, no police,' Louise piped up, giving her sister a sideways look.

'No, it's ok. We're fine, no harm done. If we get the police involved it'll be a major headache. We'll probably be at the police station half the weekend and it'll ruin your stag party,' said Sandra.

'Ok, if that's what you want,' Danny said, unconvinced by the answer. There was something off about the two women. The frightened looks on their faces had vanished quicker than he'd expected for civilians.

'Well, at least let us escort you back to the hotel,' Danny added, noticing Sandra attaching herself to Chaz.

As the women nodded, Danny spotted a couple of flyers lying in the road that must have blown out of the van as it screamed off.

"Club Desire. Gentleman's lap dancing club."

They walked back to the bar where Scott placed his glass on the table and clapped his hands. 'Well, that didn't take long. I thought you might have at least got to tomorrow before you got into some sort of fight.'

'Do us a favour and make use of those Spanish lessons, Scott, ask the barman to phone for an ambulance for that scumbag over there. Here, give him this. Make sure he understands. We were never here, ok?' Danny said, passing a fifty Euro note out of his wallet for a tip.

'Roger that, old man,' said Scott, heading inside to have a word with the barman.

When they all got back to the hotel, they headed up to their rooms on the third floor. As Chaz and Fergus said goodnight, Sandra's eyes locked with Chaz's, causing an awkward pause amongst the group that only ended when they headed down the corridor to their rooms at the opposite end of the floor to Danny, Scott and the sisters.

'Sorry if I've been a bit off. I'm still a bit shaken up. I don't suppose either of you has something strong to drink in your room to settle my nerves?' said Louise, surprising both of them by her change of character.

'Of course, my dear, I have some excellent malt whiskey. You are quite welcome to have a little sample.'

'Thank you, er …?'

'Scott, Scott Miller.'

'Thank you, Scott. Are you coming, sis?' Louise said, turning to Sandra.

'No, I've had enough excitement for one night. You go. I'm going to bed.'

'Well, you're safe now. I'll leave you to it, Scott. Good night, ladies,' said Danny, turning to head to his room.

'Danny isn't it?' Sandra said, stopping him in his tracks.

'Yes.'

'Thanks again for earlier. I don't know what we would have done if you hadn't been there.'

'You're welcome,' he replied, heading off, smiling as he heard Scott laying on his usual slick charm while escorting Louise back to his room for a nightcap.

CHAPTER 5

The phone buzzed on the marble top of the large breakfast bar, the vibration sounding like an angry bee in a matchbox. Gregory Delany stopped pacing and grabbed it before the third ring.

'Talk to me, Mendez.'

'We ran into a problem.'

'What do you mean you ran into a problem? How hard could it be? They're just two women,' Delany said, cutting Mendez short as his voice rose.

'Some wannabe hero and his friends got involved as we were grabbing them. They put three of my men in hospital with burst eardrums, broken ribs and a fractured eye socket.'

'Where is she now?' Delany ordered, with no interest in the fate of Mendez's men.

'They are back at the hotel. I have men keeping watch. We will have to grab them when they come out in the morning.'

'No, I want them tonight.'

'I can't. There are cameras, hotel security.'

'Do I need to remind you what would happen if the contents of that memory stick fell into the wrong hand?. Now get them and that stick back, tonight. Everyone has their price, bribe the hotel staff, threaten them, kill them. I don't fucking care. I just want her and the memory stick back. Now, Mendez, do you hear me? I'm flying out tomorrow. Don't let me down,' Delany was yelling by the time he hung up, slamming the phone down on the marble worktop. He poured himself another whisky into a tumbler and downed it while still holding the bottle in the other hand. A second later his pent-up fury was released as he threw the tumbler into the wall opposite, watching it explode into a million pieces.

'Fucking bitch,' he yelled at the top of his voice.

One of his men came running in at the noise, stopping dead in the doorway when his furious boss shot him an angry sideways look.

'Get someone to clean that up,' he ordered before storming out of the room.

He crossed the hall and opened the door leading to his large garage with enough room for four cars. Two men stopped what they were doing. One of them was Ken Gambit, Delany's right-hand man, and the other was one of Delany's hired muscle. Both looked Delany's way, the sleeves of their white shirts rolled up to their elbows to keep the blood on their knuckles from flicking onto the crisp white material, their suit jackets hung over a golf cart sitting against the back wall behind them. In the centre of the garage, a man tied to a chair spat blood out onto the concrete floor and wheezed as he drew in a breath.

'Please, Mr Delany, it wasn't my fault,' he gasped, looking at Gregory through the one eye that wasn't swollen shut.

'So you're saying it's my fault then?' Delany said, moving his face in close to his accountant Patrick Hopkins.

'No, no, I, er, but,' Patrick said in a terrified stutter.

'But, but, but. Was I the one who left the memory stick unattended? Was I?' Delany yelled in Patrick's face.

'No, Mr Delany.'

'I go to the trouble of having the details of a multi-million pound empire stored on two secure memory sticks, far away from any computer that could be seized, hacked or compromised, putting us all in jail. I pay a fortune to have a special biometric safe built into the wall of my fucking house to keep them safe in, and you leave one of them plugged into your laptop for that bitch to run off with, while you go off and get your fucking lunch.'

Delany's anger boiled over and he planted a right hook into Patrick's face, whipping his head back in the chair.

'Luckily for you, we know where she is, or you'd be dead by now.' Delany stood back and looked at Ken. 'Clean him up and send him home.'

'Yes boss.'

'Remember, I own you, Hopkins. You fuck up again and I'll kill you and your family,' Delany said, looking back at Patrick before heading back into the house.

He walked into the kitchen, ignoring his man clearing up the broken glass, grabbed the whisky bottle off the marble counter and headed for the stairs.

'I'm going to bed,' he shouted back over his shoulder.

CHAPTER 6

Samuel Mendez laid his phone down on the desk in his office above Club Desire. He leaned back in the chair, took a long drag on his cigarette, and let out a big cloud of smoke.

'Arlo.'

'Boss,' Arlo said, turning his head from the TV to look at Mendez as he sat in a worn leather sofa in the corner of the office.

'Find out who the night manager is at the Villa Venecia Hotel. I want to know everything about him, and get some men together. Delany won't wait. He wants the women and his damn memory stick back tonight, no matter what.'

'Tonight? It's half-past one now!'

'Just do it, Arlo. Delany is flying out tomorrow and I don't want to be the one who tells him we haven't got his bloody girlfriend and his property back, do you?' Mendez said, rubbing his forehead as he tried to ease his growing headache.

'I'll get on it straight away, boss,' Arlo said, peeling his large frame out of the chair to stand a towering six-foot-six of gym-built muscle.

'Thank you, Arlo,' Mendez said, watching his right-hand man move to the door. As he opened it, Paulo Ramos, a young bartender from downstairs, stood in the opening looking like a rabbit caught in headlights.

Arlo and Mendez just stared at him, waiting for an explanation.

'Sorry, Mr Mendez, I have the drink you asked for,' Paulo eventually said, holding up a glass in his shaking hand.

'About time. Bring it here,' Mendez said, beckoning him over.

As Paulo placed the drink on the desk, Mendez shot out a hand to grab his wrist in a steely grip.

'When you were outside the door, you didn't hear anything, did you, Paulo?' Mendez said, his voice low and calm, his grip tightening as he stared unwaveringly into Paulo's eyes.

'Er, no, Mr Mendez, nothing. I was just about to knock when the door opened,' Paulo said, physically shaking, with fear written all over his face.

Mendez held him there for a few more seconds just to reinforce the power he had over him before letting go and smiling.

'Good, too much knowledge can be hazardous for your health. Now go and get me the bottle. It's going to be a long night,' Mendez said, downing the drink in one before turning his attention to some papers on his desk, leaving Paulo to shuffle awkwardly out of the door.

A few minutes later, there was a knock at the door.

'Come,' Mendez yelled.

Mateo Guilar entered, his eye swollen nearly shut and turning a purplish-black colour.

'Mateo, come in. How's your eye? What did the hospital say?'

'It's ok, no permanent damage, a fractured cheekbone, it should heal ok on its own.'

'Good, tell me what happened. Was it Alonzo's men?' Mendez said, sitting forward.

'No, no, we were just unlucky. This one man, from England, he got involved and his friends followed him.'

'Definitely not Alonzo's men?'

'No boss, I sent Felipe to ask at the bars opposite. There were four of them, ex-army or something. The barmen heard them talking about their days in the military, which explains what happened at the van. They are here on a stag weekend. You know, shorts, stupid T-shirts, fucking Brits on the piss.'

'Ok, good, thank you, Mateo, go and get some rest,' said Mendez, relaxing back into his chair as Mateo left, passing Paulo in the hallway as he brought Mendez his bottle of drink.

CHAPTER 7

Danny woke up and showered, any thoughts of last night's trouble long gone, replaced by the weekend's festivities and his forthcoming wedding to Nikki. He gave Scott's door a knock on his way to breakfast, chuckling at Scott's frown when he looked at his pink T-shirt with "The Stag" printed on it.

'Mmm, classy. Come in, old boy, I've just got to put my shoes on. I hope you're not expecting me to wear one of those?' Scott said, turning away from the door in his short-sleeved Armani shirt and a cloud of some expensive aftershave.

'I won't, but you might have a job convincing Ferg and Chaz, Scotty boy. Whoa, ease up on the aftershave, mate, you smell like a right tart. Oh, by the way, is it safe to come in? You haven't got that Louise still tucked away in here somewhere?' Danny said with a grin.

'Of course not. I was the perfect gentleman. It was a bit weird actually. She came in, asked to use the toilet, and when she emerged she said she'd changed her mind about the drink and scurried out the door without so much as a 'goodnight'.'

'You must be losing your touch, mate. Come on, I'm starving,' Danny said, leading Scott out of the room.

They headed down the corridor towards the stairs. Danny could see a cleaning trolley outside Sandra and Louise's room. The housekeeper standing beside the trolley was gesturing and talking at a hundred miles an hour in Spanish to another housekeeper inside the room. When they drew level, Danny looked inside to see the bed sheets on the floor with all the drawers pulled out and wardrobe doors open, and no sign of the sisters or their luggage.

'Scott, ask them what happened to Sandra and Louise.'

'Right, er, let me think.'

While Scott spoke to the housekeepers in broken Spanish, Danny stuck his head inside the room. Apart from being turned over, there was no sign of the sisters.

'They don't know. The manager just told them to get the room ready for the next guest,' Scott said to Danny before smiling at the housekeepers, 'Gracias señoritas.'

Danny smiled and nodded to the ladies and exited the room. With a frown on his face, he quickened his pace, heading down the stairs to reception.

'Here we go again,' Scott muttered to himself, trying to keep up with him.

'Good morning, sir, how can I help you?' the receptionist said, seeing Danny approach the desk.

'Good morning. We were supposed to meet some friends in room 318 this morning, but when I passed their room, I saw that it's empty. Could you tell me if they've changed rooms?' Danny asked with a friendly smile.

'Let me see, sir,' the receptionist said, tapping the

keyboard on the desk. 'According to the system, the two ladies from room 318 checked out at four o'clock this morning.'

'Four? Did they say anything? Do you know why they left?' Danny said, trying his best not to come across as too insistent.

'I don't know, sir, I've only just come on shift. Er, if you wait just one minute, the night shift manager is still here, I will go and get him.'

'Thank you. I'd appreciate it,' Danny said, smiling at her.

'I say, old boy, are you sure about this? After all, it's not really any of our business, is it?' Scott said while they waited.

'I just want to make sure they are alright, Scott. Doesn't this strike you as odd, especially after last night's events?'

'Just because it's strange, it still doesn't make it any of our business,' Scott protested.

'Can I help you, sir?' came the night manager's voice behind them.

'Yes, our friends were in room 318. Apparently they checked out in the early hours of this morning. I just wondered if they said where they were going, or if they asked you to get them a taxi anywhere?' Danny said, observing the man's body language, noticing how nervous he looked, with a little trickle of sweat running down his temple as he shifted from foot to foot.

'Yes señor, they ordered a taxi to the airport. I believe they were flying home. Some kind of family emergency.'

The man looked decidedly uncomfortable, speaking fast, as if he'd rehearsed the speech in his head before-hand. Danny didn't push him further.

STEPHEN TAYLOR

'Thank you,' he said, turning away and walking towards the dining hall with Scott.

'There you are, old man, all easily explained.'

Danny didn't reply. He turned to look back at reception to see the night manager talking to someone on his mobile. The minute their eyes met, the manager turned away nervously as if he hadn't been watching him. With his mind still turning over the things that didn't add up, he headed down the stairs to the dining hall on the lower ground level.

'Oh good grief,' Scott said, spotting Chaz and Fergus tucking into breakfast in matching pink T-shirts. Fergus's had "I'm with this twat" on the front and Chaz's had "Shag me, I'm single".

The sight of the two of them made Danny laugh, despite the puzzle of the missing sisters. Heading straight for the breakfast buffet, Danny piled his plate high before taking a seat opposite Fergus and Chaz.

'You'd better line your stomach better than that, Scott, you're going to need it,' said Fergus, laughing at Scott's two croissants and a yoghurt.

'That may be, Fergus, old man, but when you are all rolling around on the floor with heart attacks from hardened arteries, I'll still be walking around as fit as a fiddle. I wonder who will be laughing then,' Scott said with a smug smile.

'Not if I kill you first, you won't,' Fergus said, holding his sausage upright on the fork so it looked like he was sticking his middle finger up.

'So what's the condemned man's plan of action?' Chaz said, ignoring Scott and Fergus.

Danny didn't answer. He was staring out of the dining room window across the hotel pool and gardens, deep in thought.

'Earth calling Danny.'

Danny turned his head slowly to face them. 'I thought we might check out that lap dancing place, Club Desire.'

'Really?' Fergus said as they all looked at Danny oddly.

'A strip club? You know I was only joking about that last night?'

'Yes Daniel, that's rather unlike you. What are you up to?' said Scott, eyeing Danny suspiciously.

'Just a healthy curiosity, we'll go after breakfast,' Danny said casually before tucking back into his breakfast.

'After breakfast? It won't be open until tonight,' Fergus said.

'I know. That's the best time to go,' Danny said, looking up and smiling.

'That's it. Come on, what's going on?' Chaz said.

Danny filled them in about the Club Desire flyer that fell out of the van the night before and Sandra and Louise's room being turned over, and their apparent check out told by the obviously nervous night manager.

'Don't you think we should raise our concerns with the police?' Scott said, shrugging when all three of them turned to look at him. 'What?'

'We've got no sisters, no evidence that someone tried to abduct or rob them, and I'm pretty sure we put three men in hospital, which would get us arrested. Look, I just want to take a look around Club Desire. I'm sure it'll come to nothing and if you want to wait at the hotel, we won't think any less of you,' Danny said to Scott.

'Now I didn't say that, did I? You can count on me. I just have to go and brush my teeth and I'll be right with you,' Scott said, excusing himself to head up to his room. He entered the bathroom and reached into his wash bag for the toothpaste and brush. As he felt around inside, his fingers felt something small and hard. When he pulled it out, a rugged 256-bit AES encryption, military-grade USB memory stick sat between his fingertips.

'How strange. Now that's a rather serious bit of kit,' Scott mumbled to himself, turning it over as he wondered how it got there.

His mind cast back to last night and Louise Benning asking to use the bathroom as soon as she entered his room, then making an excuse and leaving straight afterwards.

So what is so important about this that you'd hide it in my room, and who are you hiding it from?

'Maybe I'll have just a little peek,' Scott said to himself, heading for his laptop.

He booted it up and plugged the memory stick in. As expected it asked for an access password. Scott opened up some device interrogation software that told him all he needed to know about the memory stick.

'Mmm, someone didn't want anybody getting into this little beauty,' Scott muttered, taking the drive out of the computer and putting it in his pocket.

He closed the laptop down and headed back downstairs to join the others, their impatience at waiting for him making him forget to mention his discovery.

CHAPTER 8

High in the hills in Maylan, Alonzo Acosta walked out onto his pool terrace. He took in the panoramic views of the mountains leading all the way down to the tightly packed tall hotels and apartment buildings of Benidorm in the distance, with the deep blue Mediterranean Sea beyond. He sipped his coffee, turning his head at the sound of the electric gate opening. The black Mercedes of his right-hand man, Leo Quinn, drove around the circular drive to park next to the building.

'Morning Leo, you want a coffee?' Alonzo said as Leo stepped up onto the terrace, brushing his slicked back grey hair into place with his hand.

'Yes, thank you,' Leo said, following Alonzo into the kitchen.

'So what brings you up the hill so early in the morning?' Alonzo said, handing Leo a small cup of strong black coffee.

'I've just had some interesting information from our man inside Mendez's club.'

'What, that little creep, Paulo?'

'Yes, he says Gregory Delany's girlfriend left him. She jumped on a plane with her sister and is here in Benidorm.'

'So, what do I care about that?' Alonzo said, shrugging.

'She stole something from him when she left.'

'What?' Alonzo said, his curiosity piqued.

'An encrypted memory stick,' said Leo, pausing to take a sip of coffee.

'What's on it?'

'He doesn't know, but Delany is going crazy about it. Mendez has been running everyone around to get her and the memory stick back. They tried to grab the two sisters on the way back to their hotel, but ran into trouble with some British soldiers on a stag weekend. It ended with three of Mendez's men in the hospital. Paulo says Delany has ordered Mendez to pay the night manager off at the hotel, the Villa Venecia, so they can grab the women from their room. That's all he knows. Oh, and Delany is flying out later today.'

'What, here? Delany is coming to Benidorm?' Alonzo said, surprised.

'Yes, today.'

Alonzo put his coffee cup down and walked back out onto the pool terrace. He looked down at Benidorm in the distance, deep in thought. Leo followed and stood beside his boss without saying a word, waiting for instruction.

'Check out the hotel. Find out if Mendez got to Delany's girlfriend and sister. If he did, put men on the club, the factory and Mendez's villa. Call me as soon as you know where he's keeping them.'

'Ok,' Leo said, getting his phone out of his pocket as he turned to leave.

'And put someone at the airport. I want to know the second Delany lands. Whatever's on that memory stick, it's really important to Delany, and if it's important to him, I want it.'

Leo turned back and nodded to Alonzo before continuing to his car.

CHAPTER 9

As most clubs and bars do, Club Desire looked decidedly underwhelming in the bright morning sunshine. It was located on the corner of a busy crossroads and with all the neon signage turned off, the matt black painted building looked deserted and drab. Danny tried the door. It was locked. He looked down either side of the building, smiling to himself when he saw the driveway leading to the rear of the club.

'Go and get a drink over there. I'm going to have a peep around the back. If you see anything that looks like trouble, call me,' Danny said, turning back to the others and pointing to a bar across the road.

'Yeah, go and get a drink and call us if you see any trouble,' Fergus said, smiling back at Chaz and Scott before walking after Danny.

'Get yourself a drink, Scott, and call us if there's any trouble,' said Chaz, turning back to Scott as he walked after the others.

'What sort of trouble exactly?' Scott said, rolling his eyes.

'I don't know, just trouble,' Chaz shouted back.

'Ok children, you go and play, the grown ups will be just over here,' Scott muttered to himself as he crossed the road and took a seat outside the bar.

'What can I get you, sir?' The waiter said, setting up the last few tables ready for the day's service.

'Can I have a cappuccino please,' Scott said, looking at the time and deciding it was too early for a gin and tonic.

At the back of the club, Danny took a step out to see around the large rubbish bins into a small courtyard. The back door of the club was open, with the van from last night parked in the corner. When he moved back under cover, Fergus and Chaz were crouched beside him, grinning.

'I said wait at the bar. Did you see the van?'

'Yep,' said Fergus and Chaz in unison.

'Well, you're here now. You might as well make yourselves useful,' Danny said, giving in and nodding towards the door.

'Roger that,' they both replied, still grinning.

The three of them moved swiftly to the door, Fergus and Chaz flipping to one side while Danny tucked against the wall on the other side. He darted his head across to take a quick mental snapshot of the interior before darting away again.

Long corridor, kitchen to the left, bar and stage at the far end. Two doors off the corridor, nobody in sight.

Danny rolled around and entered, with Fergus and Chaz following close behind. They stopped when Danny took a look into the kitchen. A giant of a chef had his back to them, his arms moving as he prepped food for cooking later. He was about six foot seven and thirty stone with hands like shovels. Danny passed the doorway, beckoning

39

Fergus and Chaz to follow him further along the corridor. He paused by a door marked Privado and looked at the push button security lock. It was old and loose in the door. When he pushed it he could see a glimmer of light around its edge coming from the other side and the brass latch as it stuck out into the door frame. Danny turned to Chaz and made a twisting-a-key-in-a-lock motion before pointing at the door and moving on to look into the bar and stage area. Chaz looked at the lock and pointed towards the kitchen for Fergus, making a stabbing motion at the gap between the lock and frame. Fergus nodded and edged back towards the kitchen to get a knife.

Danny glanced into the bar and main club area. Music was playing, but not too loudly. No one was there apart from Paulo, who was busy restocking the bar fridges and shelves with bottles and cans ready for opening time.

Back in the corridor, Fergus looked into the kitchen. The huge chef still had his back to the door and was busy chopping onions and garlic for the pan sizzling on the hob in front of him. Treading carefully, Fergus slid into the kitchen, moving silently up behind the chef, who made him look like a child in comparison. He reached out and picked up a small knife from the stainless steel worktop and started walking backwards towards the door, his eyes on the giant chef as he went. He'd only moved a couple of feet when his elbow knocked into the pans hanging on hooks from a bar attached to the wall, causing a soft clang as they bumped into each other. Fergus froze, his eyes moving from the pans to the chef. The chopping stopped and the chef stood slowly upright before turning around with a large chopping knife in his hand, a curious look on his face as he took in Fergus standing in his kitchen in shorts and a T-shirt holding a small knife.

'Er, *hola*,' Fergus said, placing the little knife down before holding his palms up, adding a disarming smile as he stepped backwards towards the door.

The chef's face went from passive to enraged in a blink of the eye. He came at Fergus, swiping the large chopping knife in front of him.

'Oh shit.' Fergus shot a hand out to grab a large pan off its hook. He did a backhand swipe at the chef's knife hand, hitting the blade's metal edge with a clang before it whacked on the chef's knuckles with a dull thud.

The chef's grip loosened, and the knife flew away to the far side of the kitchen. Using the momentum of the pan swinging away from his body, Fergus twisted to put all his speed and body weight into a right-hand punch to the chef's kidneys. As he struck the giant chef, the flesh folded around his fist like he was punching dough. Seemingly unaffected, the chef grabbed Fergus around the throat with one massive hand and grabbed the belt of his shorts with the other.

'Oh shit,' Fergus croaked as the chef picked him up off the ground and hurled him across the stainless steel preparation table, knocking utensils and containers crashing and clattering to the floor as he slid off the edge and slammed into the large catering fridge.

As Fergus attempted to get up, the chef pushed the heavy stainless steel table to one side as if it weighed nothing and bent down to pick up the large chopping knife, his eyes fixing murderously on Fergus.

'Oh shit,' Fergus said again, his feet slipping on the fallen utensils as he tried to get up.

Barely on his feet and not yet fully upright, Fergus threw his arms up to defend himself, expecting to feel the cold steel blade slicing into his flesh as the chef bore down on him. Instead, there was massive clang and the chef fell to one side in slow motion like a tree being felled. In his place stood Chaz, holding the handle of a heavy wrought iron frying pan with both hands like you would a baseball bat.

'Come on, Ferg, stop pissing around with your new mate and let's get on with this,' Chaz said, dropping the pan when he saw the chef was out cold.

'Alright, I'm coming. I didn't need your help. Another couple of minutes and I would have had him,' said Fergus, grabbing the little knife for the door lock before following Chaz out of the kitchen.

'Christ, can you two make any more noise?' Danny said, coming back down the corridor.

'Don't look at me, blame Mr Michelin Star behind me,' Chaz said, manipulating the little knife through the thin gap between the lock and frame while Fergus shrugged at Danny. Before Danny could say anything else, the latch slid back, and the door popped open.

'Bingo,' Chaz said with a grin.

CHAPTER 10

Outside in the sunshine, Scott sipped his coffee while checking and answering some of the many business emails he got every day on his phone. He was so engrossed he didn't notice a black Mercedes pulling to a stop a little way up the road. Chavez and Daunte, two of Alonzo's men, got out and walked towards the bar he was sitting in. They eyed Club Desire intently as they approached, taking a seat at the table next to Scott before ordering two espresso coffees. As he finished typing, Scott felt something hard in his pocket. He reached in and pulled out the USB memory stick. He looked at it closely, turning it over in his fingers under the bright sunlight.

I'd forgotten about you. What secrets might you hold then?

'So what does the boss want us to do if we see these English women?' Daunte said in Spanish.

Scott stopped twiddling the memory stick when he heard them mention English women.

'He said to call him, and don't let them out of our sight.

He was more interested in some stupid memory stick one of them is supposed to have,' replied Chavez.

'What's on it?'

'I don't know, but whatever it is, it belongs to Gregory Delany and he wants it back really badly. Which means Acosta wants to get hold of it, really badly.'

'Shit, Gregory Delany, the cocaine king himself. This could get messy,' Daunte said, glancing across at Scott who folded his hand around the memory stick and pretended to look around absentmindedly.

'Good morning, lovely day for it,' Scott said in a loud patronising voice, as if he was a holiday maker who didn't speak any Spanish.

'Fucking English idiots,' Chavez said in Spanish before the two men turned away to watch the club.

Moving slowly, Scott put his hand down and slid the memory stick back into his pocket. Eyeing the two hard-looking men out of the corner of his eye, he picked up his phone and typed a message.

CHAPTER 11

With Danny in the lead, the three of them moved silently up the stairs to the first floor. They spread out on the landing at the top, listening at each door before opening it. The first one was a large dressing room full of skimpy costumes for the dancers who would work there much later on. The next door led to the toilets, leaving a third door across the landing. Danny moved up to it and placed his ear on the wooden surface. He could hear voices talking quietly with only the odd Spanish word comprehensible. Danny tapped his ear and held up two fingers to Chaz and Fergus to indicate two people inside. They nodded back, falling in behind Danny as he counted three, two, one on his fingers before he entered the room, stepping forward from the doorway to let Chaz and Fergus fan out on either side of him.

Mateo, the man Danny had punched in the face, and the driver from the night before were kneeling in the middle of the room, busily ripping the lining out of the two pink suitcases belonging to the Benning sisters. At the sound of the door opening they stopped their search for the memory stick and looked up at Danny, Fergus and Chaz, a mixture of surprise and confusion written across their faces at the "I'm with this twat", "Shag me, I'm single" and "The Stag," pink T-shirts. A split second later recognition kicked in, followed by fear.

Already in motion as Mateo's hand went for the gun inside his jacket, Danny lunged forward and planted a lightning-fast right hook to the side of Mateo's face that wasn't swollen and covered in a blackish-blue bruise. His head whipped back, pulling his body with it to slap back down onto the sisters' clothes scattered around the office floor. Jumping forward, Danny thumped his knee down onto Mateo's chest and reached inside his jacket. Pulling out an HK45 compact pistol, he locked his arm out in front of him so the barrel of the gun sat inches away from the driver's face.

'Do you have a gun on you?' Danny growled

Javier nodded, pointing a finger towards his jacket without lowering his hands. Danny reached in and pulled another HK out by the grip and tossed it to Chaz.

'Where are the women these suitcases belong to?' he said, with a look that said he'd shoot without a second thought.

The driver threw his hands up higher while Mateo groaned under Danny's knee.

'They have them at the *fábrica*, er, how you say, factory. Please don't shoot.'

'*Callarse, Javier*,' Mateo grunted, telling Javier to shut up.

Danny turned and smacked the butt of the handgun down onto the bridge of Mateo's nose with a sickening crunch, snapping the gun back up to point at Javier's face while Mateo shrieked in pain.

'He's definitely still got it,' said Fergus, sitting on the edge of Mendez's desk to watch.

'Yeah, he always did have a flair for the dramatic,' replied Chaz, stifling a yawn as he stood next to him.

'What and where is this factory, and what do they want with the women?' Danny said, pulling the slide back on the gun to cock the hammer, ready to fire.

'Ok, ok, I will tell you. It is a *fabrica de helados*, er, ice cream factory, *Helado de Frutas Mendez*. It's on an industrial estate in Finestrat on the edge of town.'

'And the women, what do you want with the women?' Danny said, feeling his phone buzz in his pocket as he lifted and then thumped his knee down onto Mateo's chest to emphasise he meant business, making him grunt in pain.

'The blonde one is Gregory Delany's girlfriend. She took something of his, a memory stick, and he wants it and her back. That's all I know,' said Javier, looking nervously between Danny, Chaz and Fergus.

'Gregory Delany, who is he?' Danny demanded, bringing Javier's attention back to him.

'He's the big boss. He runs everything, import, export, distribution, everything goes through Delany.'

'Import and export of what?' Danny said, noting the look of surprise on Javier's face when he realised they didn't know who he was talking about.

'Cocaine, Gregory Delany is the cocaine king.'

'Let's go,' Danny said, turning to Chaz and Fergus.

'What do we do with these couple of idiots?' Fergus said, hopping off Mendez's desk.

Danny looked around him, bending down to pick up a

pair of tights and leggings off the floor. 'We'll tie them up, gag them and lock them in the toilets across the hall. Hopefully no one will discover them until after we've got the girls back.'

'Roger that, just like old times,' Chaz said with a grin.

'Yeah it's a shame Smudge isn't here, he'd have loved this,' said Fergus, thinking of their lost comrade.

'Yeah, he would have,' said Danny, spotting Sandra and Louise's passports sticking out from underneath the pile of clothes. Picking them up, he put them in his pocket. Feeling his phone, he remembered it buzzing and pulled it out to have a look. A message from Scott filled the screen.

"FYI, bad guys turned up looking for the sisters. They are sitting right next to me, staring at the club. Oh, and I might inadvertently have something they are all looking for."

"What thing?" Danny messaged back.

"A memory stick. I think Louise hid it in my room last night."

'Scott's got the memory stick,' Danny said to Chaz and Fergus, dragging the tied-up and gagged Javier and Mateo across the hall to the toilets.

'What? How the fuck has Scott got the memory stick?' said Fergus, snapping the handle off the toilet door so nobody could open it.

'Louise hid it in his room last night. Come on, let's get out of here.' Danny said, texting another message to Scott.

"Leave now. Start walking back down the road. We'll catch you up in a minute."

'Oh shit, we might have a teeny little problem to deal with before we go,' said Fergus, as they headed down the stairs and out into the corridor.

'Ferg, what?' Danny said, looking back at him.

'Er, that,' Fergus said, pointing into the kitchen.

'Oh, for fuck's sake,' Danny said, looking in to see the giant chef lying unconscious on the floor. 'Ok, let's lock him in the food chiller. Come on, you two get his arms.'

Chaz and Fergus grabbed an arm each, groaning as they strained to pick him up off the floor. Danny grabbed his legs and lifted. The veins popped on his neck as if he was doing a deadlift in the gym.

'Jesus, how much does this bastard weigh?' grunted Chaz.

They'd got him half in and half out of the chiller when the barman, Paulo, walked into the kitchen.

Danny dropped the legs and whipped the gun out, pointing it at Paulo's face, while Chaz and Fergus dropped their end and poked their heads out of the chiller to see what was going on.

'Whoa, no, wait. I'm just a barman, I've seen nothing, ok?' shouted Paulo, shooting his hands up.

There was a tense silence and nobody moved as painfully slow seconds ticked by.

'Do you know where the factory is, Helado de Frutas? The industrial estate in Finestrat. Do you know where it is?' Danny finally said.

'Sí, er, yes, I know where it is,' Paulo said nervously.

'Do you have a car?'

'Sí, it is out the back.'

'Good, come here and help us move him into the cooler,' Danny said, tucking the gun away so he could grab a leg.

After locking the chef in the walk-in food cooler, they exited the club by the back door and stood outside in the small courtyard.

49

'Where's your car?' Danny said.

'It's over there,' Paulo pointed to a car tucked in the corner of the courtyard.

'You've gotta be kidding,' Chaz said, following his gaze.

CHAPTER 12

Scott's phone buzzed with Danny's incoming message. He read it then tucked it into his pocket and got up to leave. Alonzo's men paid him no attention, their focus directed towards the club across the road. Scott walked behind them and out of the bar. He moved behind Chavez and Daunte's black Mercedes before crossing the road to walk away from the club down the road.

Daunte watched him head away from them, more out of boredom than suspicion. Just as his eyes left Scott and tracked back to the front of the club, a tiny, bright yellow, two door Seat Arosa driven by a small Spanish man emerged from the access road to the rear of the club, with two large men squeezed in the back and another in the front, all with pale complexions and pink T-shirts. The T-shirt worn by the man sitting in the front passenger seat had "The Stag" written on it in large letters. With its suspension low at the rear, the little car revved as it turned onto the road. It only drove a little way before stopping beside Scott. Danny jumped out and folded the passenger seat forward before pushing a complaining Scott in between Chaz and Fergus. As he turned to get back in, Daunte spotted what looked like a gun tucked into the back of Danny's shorts.

'Hey Chavez.'

'What?'

'Didn't the boss say when Mendez's men tried to grab Delany's girlfriend a bunch of British soldiers on a stag weekend stopped them?'

'Yeah, two of them are still in hospital, fucking amateurs. Why?'

Daunte tapped him on the shoulder and pointed to the tiny car just as Danny slammed the door shut and it pulled away. The suspension was crushed to its limit at the back with the weight of four British stag weekenders and a Spanish bartender squeezed inside.

'I'll drive. You call Leo, see what he wants us to do,' said Chavez, tucking some Euros under the coffee cup to pay for the drinks.

The two of them ran to the car, spinning it around in the road before taking off in the direction of the bright yellow Seat.

'Boss, we've just seen the British soldiers that stopped Mendez's men last night. They've just left Club Desire in some piece of shit yellow Seat,' Daunte said on the phone.

'Yellow Seat? Did you see a Spanish man, skinny, early twenties, curly hair?' Leo said back.

'Yeah, he was driving. I can see them up ahead. What do you want me to do?'

'Just follow them. Don't let them see you, ok? Call me as soon as you know where they're going.'

'Ok boss,' said Daunte, hanging up and turning to

Chavez. 'Boss wants us to tail them and let him know where they go.'

'Well, it's not like they're going to lose us, is it?' Chavez said, pulling back so he didn't get too close to the slow moving Seat.

CHAPTER 13

'Bump!' Danny called out at the approaching speed bump.

'Argh.'

'Jesus.'

'Bloody hell, old man, are you trying to kill us?' complained Scott, Chaz and Fergus as the rear suspension bottomed out and jolted their spines.

'Stop complaining,' Danny grinned, turning back in his seat to look at them, his grin dropping at the sight of the black Mercedes forty metres behind them. 'Paulo, take the next left.'

'But that's not the way to—' Paulo said back, puzzled.

'Just do it,' said Danny, interrupting him.

'Ok.' Paulo turned down a side street that led away from the high apartment blocks and tall hotels into an estate of large villas and houses tucked behind gates and high walls.

'What is it?' Fergus said, trying to crane his head while being sandwiched in the back.

'I'll know any second now,' Danny replied, his eyes

locked on the junction behind them until he saw the black Mercedes turn after them. 'We've got a tail. Scott, did you get anything from the guys in the bar?'

'Absolutely. The work for somebody called Acosta. I assume he's a rival to the owner of the memory stick everyone's looking for. A man called Gregory Delany, AKA the cocaine king.'

'Gregory Delany, that's Louise's ex-boyfriend,' Danny said, turning his head to check on the Mercedes still following forty metres back. Turning forward again, he could see the road bent sharply to the left up ahead. 'Paulo, as soon as I say, speed up, ok?'

'Sí, ok,' Paulo said, looking nervously in the mirror at Acosta's men in the following Mercedes, secretly worried about being caught in between the Alonzo's man who paid him for information on Mendez, the men in his car and Mendez himself.

'Now, go, go, go!' Danny said, the second the curve of the road put them out of sight of the following Mercedes.

The bend kept on going as they sped up, Chaz, Fergus and Scott in the back groaning as the car banged over another speed bump. It eventually straightened out after a hundred and eighty degree turn, leaving them heading back towards the main road they'd turned off.

'There, pull in behind them,' Danny pointed to a car driving in through the electric gates of their villa.

As Paulo braked and yanked the steering wheel, Danny looked back, relieved to see the Mercedes hadn't emerged from the bend in the road, before they shot through the closing electric gates, skidding to a stop inches from the owner's car. The surprised homeowner got out and stared dumbfounded at the five men squashed into the little car as they looked back at him from all different angles.

'Paulo, tell him we're sorry, we got the wrong house,' Danny said, winding the window down to stick his head out. As he looked back towards the gate he heard the Mercedes accelerating past as it attempted to catch the car they thought had got away from them.

By the time the owner opened the gate and they reversed out, the Mercedes was nowhere to be seen. A few minutes later they were back on the main road heading towards the industrial estate.

'Sorry,' said Fergus, sandwiched in the back.

'What for? Oh, you dirty bastard,' Chaz said as the smell of Fergus's fart hit his nostrils.

'Good lord that smells. Open a window, Daniel, before I pass out,' shouted Scott, trying to lean forward to get some air.

'I can't help it. It's all the foreign food,' Fergus said apologetically.

'Foreign food! You've only had breakfast, and that was a full English,' Danny said, lowering the front window.

'Yeah, but we're in Spain, so it was a Spanish full English breakfast, wasn't it?' Fergus protested.

They turned in by the retail shops at the front of the industrial estate and worked their way towards the ice cream factory on the far side.

'Where is it?' Danny asked Paulo.

'It's the last building, just up ahead by that red lorry,' Paulo said, nodding towards a factory unit on the edge of the estate.

'Ok, pull over here.'

Paulo did as he was told, sitting nervously as he waited for whatever was going to happen next.

'Can I trust you, Paulo?' Danny said, turning to look at him.

'*Sí*, yes, you can trust me,' Paulo answered quickly.

'If we let you go, you're not going to phone your boss and tell him we're here, are you?'

'No, no, I won't say anything, I promise.'

Danny looked into Paulo's eyes, staring at him for an uncomfortably long time.

'Ok, I believe you. Take a slow drive back to the club and let the chef out of the food cooler. Oh, and there's two more men locked in the toilet upstairs. Tell them you popped out for a minute and found them when you came back. You didn't see any of us, okay?'

Paulo nodded.

Danny got out and folded the seat forward so Chaz, Fergus and Scott could unfold themselves from the back, groaning and stretching until they were finally standing upright. Shutting the door, Danny bent down and looked in.

'Hey Paulo, you look like a good kid, you might want to think about finding a job with a better employer. Good luck.'

'Thank you,' Paulo said, turning the little car around and driving away.

'Right, Staff, what's the plan?' Fergus said to Danny, reverting to how they addressed him as Staff Sergeant in their SAS days.

'Save the girls, get some ice cream, then get back on the beers,' Danny said matter-of-fact as the four of them started walking towards the factory.

CHAPTER 14

'What do you mean you lost them? They were in a fucking Seat Arosa, for Christ's sake, Chavez,' Leo growled down the phone.

'I'm sorry, boss, we lost sight of them as they went around a corner and they just vanished,' said Chavez, hoping Leo didn't have a full scale meltdown or he'd be doing shit jobs for the foreseeable future.

Leo was just about to explode when Paulo Ramos drove past him in the packed Seat Arosa, pulling up twenty metres ahead of them. He watched Danny, Fergus and Chaz pull themselves from the tiny car in shorts and bright pink T-shirts with the different slogans written on them, followed by Scott in his cream trousers and Armani short-sleeved shirt. They stretched and chatted as Paulo left, then headed in the direction of the ice cream factory, the bulge of a handgun tucked in the back of the shorts of two of them, barely disguised by the T-shirt pulled over the top.

'Forget about it. You and Daunte get your arses over here. Now. Something's about to go down.'

'Yes boss.'

Leo hung up, his eyes glued to Danny and the others. 'Who the fuck are these idiots? And why is that slippery little shit Paulo driving them around?' he said to Tomás in the driving seat beside him.

'I don't know, but they've got some balls if they're going to take on Mendez's distribution factory.'

'They just came from Club Desire. Perhaps they are working for Mendez.'

'Then why put three of his men in the hospital when they tried to get the women?' said Tomás, leaning forward to watch Danny and the others getting closer to the factory.

'True. They're English, maybe Delany's men? No, that doesn't make sense either,' said Leo, shaking his head.

'Perhaps the ex-girlfriend's paying them to protect her.'

'Maybe, or maybe there's someone else involved, maybe she's done a deal for whatever is on that memory stick with one of Delany's rivals,' said Leo, looking at the driver, both of them instantly thinking his last idea made more sense than any of the others.

Leo's phone rang as his mind spun through the list of anyone in the game big enough to take on Delany and Mendez.

'Yes,'

'It's Santiago at Alicante airport. I've just seen Mendez and Arlo in the arrivals hall, and a plane from the UK touched down a little while ago. Delany must be on it.'

'Ok, thanks. Text me just before they leave the airport, ok?'

'Ok boss.'

Leo hung up and looked out through the front windscreen as Danny and the others in the distance stood opposite the factory, studying it.

'Shit, Delany's just landed,' Leo said, looking at his watch.

'Looks like things are going to get really interesting around here. How long have we got?'

'Not long, forty minutes perhaps. Chavez and Daunte will be here in a minute. We'll just have to sit it out. If they come out with the girlfriend before Mendez and Delany get here, we'll ambush them and grab her.'

'If they come out,' said Tomás, looking doubtful they would.

'Yeah, if they come out,' Leo muttered to himself.

His phone buzzed while he pondered his options.

"Delany's just left the airport in a hurry with Arlo and Mendez and four of his men."

'Shit, it might be less than forty minutes. Where the fuck are Chavez and Daunte?'

'Here they come now, boss,' Tomás said, turning in the seat to see Chavez tearing up the road behind them in the Mercedes before braking hard to stop behind them.

'Good, go and tell them what's happening, and tell them to have their guns ready and wait for my order.'

'Yes boss.'

As soon as Tomás was out of the car, Leo got back on the phone to call Alonzo.

CHAPTER 15

'Ok, so what do you reckon? Front door it, or find another way in?' Danny said, looking across the road at the factory building.

'I say we sneak around the back, force our way in through a fire escape, knock a few chaps out and rescue the women before hightailing it out the way we came,' said Scott excitedly taking up a Jiu Jitsu stance he'd learned from one of the five lessons he'd taken before he got bored with it.

The three ex-soldiers all turned to look at him. Chaz raised his eyebrows, while Fergus just shook his head.

'Really, Scott, just knock a few chaps out. You're staying out here, you can keep watch again,' Danny said, turning his attention back to the factory and a group of men in white coats and hairnets standing down the side of the factory having a cigarette break by an open fire exit door and some external metal shipping containers.

'I'm not staying out here by myself. Anything could happen. Anyway, which one of you geniuses is going to ask where Louise and Sandra are in Spanish? Hmm, *no tan listo eres,'* Scott said with a smug grin before adding, 'That's Spanish for, you're not so smart are you, by the way.'

'Can I kill him? Please let me kill him,' Fergus said, giving Scott a look.

'Ok, you can come, but keep behind us and do exactly as we say,' said Danny, giving in.

'Roger that, good buddy,' Scott said with a grin.

'Jesus Christ. Give me your gun, Ferg, I'll do him myself,' said Chaz.

'Oi, knock it off, you lot. Scott, I've told you before, it's just 'roger'. Now, see the four workers having a smoking break?'

'Aye, I'm liking your thinking,' said Fergus.

'Me too,' agreed Chaz.

'Well, would somebody like to fill me in on what you're thinking?' protested Scott.

'You keep behind us, Scott, we're going to ask those gentlemen politely for their factory uniforms and walk straight inside undetected.'

'Oh, right, well why didn't you just say so?' said Scott, tucking in behind them as they moved across the road and swiftly down the side of the factory.

As they approached, the workers looked up, a mixture of curiosity and apprehension written on their faces. Danny, Chaz, and Fergus played the part of drunk stags, laughing and staggering around as if they'd been on a bender. When they reached them, they switched in a blink of an eye, Danny and Fergus pulling the guns from behind them and indicating for the men to move over to the storage containers. Chaz lifted the handles and pulled open the heavy metal door, pleased to see the container was mostly empty, apart from some old pieces of machinery no longer needed on the production line.

'In,' Danny said, hustling them in first, before following and closing the door just enough to keep prying eyes out while letting a wedge of Spanish sunshine inside so they could see.

'Scott, tell them to take off the coats and hairnets,' said Danny.

'Right, let me see, er, *quitate el abrigo y la redecilla*,' Scott said, working through the words in his head.

'I speak English. We are not Spanish, me and Mihal are Romanian, Omar is Moroccan, and José is Columbian,' said one of the men, unbuttoning his white coat and taking it off while the others did the same.

'What's your name?' Danny asked.

'Luka.'

'Are all the workers immigrants in the factory?'

'Yes, everyone apart from the boss men. Mr Mendez gives us accommodation and pays us money to send home to our family. In return, we don't ask questions.'

'Questions about what?' Danny asked.

'About what goes on in the room at the rear of the factory. Vehicles come and go to the loading bay, men come and go, then pallets of the ice cream packages come out and go onto the delivery trucks with the ice cream we package up in the factory. It's guarded. None of us are allowed in there, only Mendez's men.'

'Have you seen two women here today, British, like us?'

Luka looked around nervously before nodding. 'The big man, Arlo, and two of Mendez's men took them into the packing room this morning. I haven't seen them leave.'

'Thank you Luka, we're going to lock you in now.

63

Someone will let you out soon. Just tell them we made you get in here at gunpoint and you'll be fine.'

'The women, I hope you get them out. They looked scared. I have a family. They would want me to help them,' said Luka.

Danny gave him a nod before pushing the door shut and pulling the heavy metal handle across to lock it shut. The four of them went in through the open fire door, white catering coats done right up and blue hairnets pulled down over their hair. They moved through the conveyor belts and a sea of stainless steel pipes and containers that fed the machines pumping different flavours of ice creams into their various containers. As Luka had said, they got sideward glances from the immigrant workers as they moved towards the rear of the factory, but their eyes soon flicked back to their jobs, none of them willing or wanting to challenge them.

A large set of double doors separating the sterile manufacturing part of the factory from the dispatch warehouse opened as they approached. Chaz, Fergus, and Danny turned on the spot to disappear behind a pallet full of ice cream containers. Looking back, Danny jumped out and grabbed Scott by the collar as he stood looking around aimlessly, pulling him out of sight as a forklift reversed through. It swivelled on the spot and picked up a pallet full of ice cream before disappearing back though the doors in a mist of super cold air from -18°C of the distribution warehouse.

'Let's go,' Danny said, moving out to the double doors.

'Tally ho,' Scott said, following excitedly, 'What?' he added when Fergus looked back at him, frowning.

Pushing the door open enough to get a look inside, Danny could only see two workers loading a lorry with the pallet from the forklift. A guard in a thermal coat and thermal trousers stood on the far side, rubbing his gloved hands together against the cold. Danny could make out the bulge of a gun under his jacket. He looked bored as he stood guard outside the doors to the room at the rear of the factory. Because he was cold, he had the jacket zipped up tight and wouldn't be able to get his gun out in a hurry. Neatly stacked pallets of ice cream stood along the back wall of the distribution warehouse waiting to be dispatched onto trucks for delivery. With the bored guard more occupied in keeping warm and watching the men loading the truck, Danny scooted across to the pallets, beckoning the others across behind him. They moved along the gap between the pallets and the back wall, hidden from sight, stopping behind the last pallet while Danny stuck his head around to see where the guard was. He was only a few metres away, his back to them as he watched the men pushing ice cream pallets into the back of a refrigerated truck with a pallet loader. Slipping the white catering coat off, Danny folded it in half and held the ends tight in each hand.

'Stay here,' he said to the others.

Running forward, Danny flicked the folded coat over the guard's head, snapping it tight around his face, blinding and gagging the man in an instant as he dragged him backwards off his feet. The man threw his hands up, clawing at the material wrapped tightly over his face as Danny pulled him behind the stacked pallets and onto the floor. Chaz and Fergus immediately moved into action, Chaz grabbing his arm while Fergus punched his material covered face repeatedly until the guy stopped moving. Unzipping the guy's thermal jacket, Fergus took his gun out and tucked it in the waistband of his shorts before covering it with his coat. Leaving the man unconscious on the floor, Danny slid the coat back on and the four of them moved swiftly to the doors leading to the restricted part of the factory. The three ex-SAS soldiers moved to either side of the doors, their guns out ready while Scott stood behind Fergus, steamy breaths coming from their mouths in the freezing warehouse. Pushing the door open a crack, Danny moved across just far enough to get a look inside.

CHAPTER 16

'So where is she?' Delany growled the second they were in the car.

'We have her and her sister at the ice cream factory,' Mendez answered calmly.

'And you haven't found the memory stick yet?'

'No, we searched the room and their belongings, but it wasn't there. I would have forced her to tell us where it was, but you said no one was to touch her.'

'That's right, she's mine, I own her. I'll soon get her to talk. Then I'll take her back home where she belongs,' said Delany, his voice quiet as he looked out the window in thought.

A split second later he snapped out of it and turned back to Mendez. 'How's distribution? No more problems with chancer Alonzo?'

'It's fine. Alonzo's not a problem. The new sterile room and the heat seal and wax dip make the produce undetectable to the sniffer dogs at the border controls.'

'Talk me through it,' Delany said. It was more of an order than a request.

'The cocaine comes in from your Sudanese supplier via my man in Algeria. It goes into a room at the factory, which is hermetically sealed. The workers cut it, weigh it and package it in heat sealed bags before sending them through a chemical wash to get rid of any traces of cocaine on the outside of the bags. The men in the cutting room never enter the packing room, so there's no chance of air or touch contamination that could be smelled by sniffer dogs or detected by a wipe test. Once the cocaine packages come out of the wash, they get dipped in wax to make sure they are 100% sealed before emerging outside of the cutting room in the packaging area. The packers then place them in the bottom of the marked containers and cover them with a layer of ice cream, then they get shipped out all across Europe.'

'Excellent, I look forward to a full tour once we have taken care of present business. How long until we get there?' Delany asked, eager to get on with things.

'It's not far now, fifteen, maybe twenty minutes.'

CHAPTER 17

The rear section of the factory was split into three sections. A large prefabricated room made of sealed UPVC sections and double-glazed windows ran across the far end. It was empty apart from rows of stainless steel tables with weighing scales and equipment to cut and seal up cocaine bricks. On the far side of the room, a large double door airlock was joined to the factory's rear fire escape door so that workers and deliveries could enter and exit without coming into the sterile packing room. A steel staircase went up in front of the room, leading to offices built on a mezzanine floor over the top. Danny could see shadows and figures moving around inside and guessed that was where they were holding Sandra and Louise. Four men worked in the packing area ahead of him, two taking blocks of cocaine as they came out of the wax dipping machine on a conveyor belt. They placed them into rows of ice cream containers where another man covered them with ice cream, before the fourth sealed and stacked them onto pallets, placing a marked label on the side of the pallet.

'Four just inside, Chaz, you cover them while me and Fergus search the offices for the sisters,' Danny said, pulling back from the door.

'Roger that,' replied Chaz, while Fergus nodded.

'I say, Daniel, what shall I do?' said Scott, his face appearing from behind Fergus.

'Just stay close to Chaz and try not to do anything stupid,' Danny said, a little impatiently.

'Bit rude,' Scott mumbled to himself.

Ignoring Scott, Danny turned back to the door. 'Go on three. One, two, three.'

Danny pushed the doors hard and moved through with Chaz and Fergus following through behind him, their guns up.

'Get down on the floor, hands behind your head,' he said, waving his hand at the floor.

The surprised men didn't move, just looked at them blankly.

'*Tirate al suelo,*' Scott said smugly, smiling when they got on the floor.

Leaving Scott and Chaz, Danny and Fergus ran to the stairs, taking them two at a time, not wanting anyone inside the offices to see what was happening before they entered.

'Go,' Danny said, pulling the door open sharply for Fergus to charge in ahead of him.

Sandra and Louise sat on a black leather sofa on the far side, guarded by two men, one on a chair in the corner and the other behind an office desk. They both reached for their guns, but stopped in their tracks when Danny and Chaz locked their arms, pointing a gun firmly in each man's direction.

'You two ok? They didn't hurt you?' Danny said to

Louise and Sandra without taking his eyes off the chubby guy behind the desk.

'No, no, we're ok,' Sandra answered, her voice surprisingly calm.

'Good, stand up and get behind me. We're leaving.'

'Hey, stupid English, do you have any idea whose place this is? You're dead men, you know that,' the guy behind the desk said, staring at Danny defiantly.

'You open your mouth again, fat boy, and I'll put a bullet in you. Now pull your gun out slowly. That's it, the butt between your fingers. Pass it over, now,' Danny growled, moving in closer, his gun pointing unwaveringly at the man's forehead.

He didn't move for a few seconds in an act of defiance, eventually relenting to do as Danny demanded, pulling the gun out between his thumb and forefinger before sliding it across the desk. Danny took it while Fergus removed the other guard's gun. With Louise and Sandra behind them, they backed out of the office and headed down the stairs.

CHAPTER 18

'Boss,' said Tomás, his eyes on the rear view mirror.

Leo bobbed his head down to see the reflection of two cars approaching fast in the wing mirror.

'Shit,' said Leo as Mendez, Arlo and Delany drove past in the first car, with a bunch of hard-looking men following in the second car.

They flew up the road, braking hard to stop in front of the factory.

'That's it. We're out of time, they're dead men and Delany will have his girlfriend and memory stick back. Should we go?' Tomás said to Leo.

'I'll call the boss and see what he wants us to do,' Leo said, reaching into his jacket for his phone without taking his eyes off the men getting out of the cars outside the factory.

They looked up and down the road for potential threats before opening the car doors for Delany, Mendez and Arlo, standing back out of the way as their bosses walked past them into the factory as if they didn't exist.

'So that's the great Delany. The cocaine king himself. He doesn't look that scary to me,' said Tomás, leaning forward to get a better look.

'Looks can be deceiving, Tomás. There's plenty of men buried in the foundations of buildings that said the same thing,' Leo said, hitting the call button on Alonzo's contact.

'Leo, what's going on?' came Alonzo's voice before the phone got a full ring in.

'We're too late, Mr Acosta. Mendez has just shown up with Delany. What do you want us to do?'

'And the Englishmen haven't come out?'

'No sir.'

'Shit, stay there and keep watch. Phone me when they come out. I want to know if they have the women and where they go.'

'Yes sir,' Leo said, hanging up.

'What did he say?' asked Tomás.

'We're to sit tight and see who comes out.'

CHAPTER 19

oving through the doors of the restricted area into the distribution warehouse, Danny and Fergus's eyes quickly scanned the area before their guns snapped across to lock on the workers still loading the delivery truck. The men froze to the spot with their hands up. They looked like the workers from the front of the factory. Immigrants from somewhere in the world worse off than here, frightened and worn down by life, certainly no threat to them. Danny and Fergus continued to the doors separating the distribution warehouse from the factory floor, while Scott moved behind them with Sandra and Louise. Chaz was the last to leave the restricted area of the factory, walking backwards into the distribution warehouse while moving his gun from the two men emerging onto the stairs from the offices, and the four packers by the pallets. The six men converged at the bottom of the stairs, keeping their distance while glaring angrily at Chaz as he disappeared through the doors before walking quickly across the warehouse to join the others. Danny pushed the door to the factory floor open, his eyes immediately locking with Mendez, Delany and Arlo as they entered the factory on the far side.

'Fuck, back it up,' Danny said, pulling the door shut just as Mendez shouted something and the three men reached inside their jackets for guns.

'What is it?' said Scott.

'Bad guys coming this way. Quick, everyone, into the delivery truck,' Danny shouted, running over to a broken pallet propped against the wall. Yanking the top plank of wood off, Danny shoved it through the handles on the warehouse doors before turning to run after the others.

'Chaz, you drive. Ferg, cover up front. We'll get in the back.'

'Roger that,' replied Chaz, waving the frightened workers out of the way. They hopped down from the raised loading bay and pulled the truck door open, grabbing the surprised truck driver and yanking him out of the cab. Danny, Scott and the sisters jumped in the back of the half-loaded truck, moving as far back as they could go while Danny turned to stare down the sights of his gun at the doors to the factory floor. They opened a few inches before locking and creaking on the plank of wood as it took the strain of Arlo's pushing. The truck's engine fired up a second later, moving out of the loading bay to let the clear plastic curtain drop behind them, keeping the hot air out of the chilled warehouse. Just before moving out of sight, Danny heard an almighty crash followed by the distorted image of Arlo through the plastic as he drove a forklift through the warehouse doors, ripping one off its hinges and shattering the plank wedged between the handles.

'Shit, cars! Hang on,' Chaz yelled, seeing Mendez's cars parked one behind the other across the exit to the road.

'Hold on to something,' Fergus banged on the bulkhead behind him and shouted.

Unable to hear them through the refrigerated truck's insulation and the racket coming in from the open back doors, Danny, Scott and the sisters all flew towards the cab as Chaz smashed the truck between the two parked cars, spinning the two lumps of twisted metal out of the way before snaking down the road. Danny slipped and stumbled around on cartons of ice cream before finding his feet to take a look out the back to see Mendez and Delany's men running into the road to look their way. As Chaz drove the truck around a corner and out of sight, Danny saw Delany, Mendez and Arlo run in front of his men. He was too far away to know what was being said, but by the way Delany was moving and waving his hands around, Danny could tell he was going ballistic.

'Oh, bloody hell. This was a brand new shirt,' Scott whinged, making Danny turn around to see him trying to wipe chocolate ice cream off his Armani shirt.

'You should have worn the T-shirt, mate,' Danny said, taking the white catering coat and hairnet off to show his pink T-shirt with "The Stag" printed on it. 'You ok, ladies?' he continued, moving over to Sandra and Louise as they lay in a pile of arms and legs over cartons of ice cream.

'Argh, er, yeah,' said Sandra, taking Danny's hand as he pulled her upright.

'Thank you so much, you saved us again,' said Louise, grabbing onto a pallet of ice cream as the truck rocked and moved about.

'You are quite welcome, my dear, but I don't think you've been entirely honest with us,' said Scott, pulling the memory stick out of his pocket and waggling it in his hand.

'Yes, I know, I'm sorry. I thought if I had something on him, he would leave me alone. He's never going to leave me alone. The only way to stop a man like that is to kill him,' Louise said, her face deadly serious.

'Now, now, I'm sure it won't come to that. Once we get somewhere safe, we can work on a way out of this mess,' Scott said, slightly taken aback by her reaction.

'But why would you? You don't know me. Oh god, you want money, that's it, you want money. I don't have any.'

'Whoa, whoa, calm down, we don't want your money, ok. We just want to help,' said Danny with a reassuring smile.

'Now you've helped us, he will come for you too. The only way out of this is to kill him,' Louise replied solemnly.

Danny didn't answer. Something about her response didn't seem natural. It felt planned, coercive. The thought disappeared when his phone started ringing with Nikki's caller ID on it.

CHAPTER 20

L eo sat in the car, bored and irritated. The windows were open, but the midday sun was heating the car up like an oven. Sweat trickled down his and Tomás's faces as they continued to watch Mendez's men standing beside the cars parked outside the factory. They both jumped when a Helado de Frutas Mendez delivery truck came out of nowhere, bursting through the two cars in front of the factory, obliterating the front of one car and the rear of the other in a shower of shattered plastic and glass crystals. The truck bounced up and down with the impact before leaning precariously as it turned to head in Leo's direction. It snaked along the road looking like it was going to hit him until the driver finally got the truck under control and hurtled past on the other side of the road.

'What the fuck?' said Tomás, gobsmacked.

'Shit. Go, go, go, Tomás. Get after them,' Leo shouted.

Tomás quickly started the car and crunched it into gear, stamping on the accelerator while locking the steering wheel to spin the car a full one-eighty. Revving the engine, Tomás flew past Chavez, with Leo shouting out the window for them to follow. Doing as he was told, Chavez spun the car around and sped off after Leo and the truck.

CHAPTER 21

'Fuck. Bastards. Someone better explain to me what the fuck just happened or I swear to God there's going to be murders. Samuel?' Delany yelled at Mendez, his face bright red as he stood in the middle of the road watching the truck disappear around the corner in the distance. A few seconds later, two black cars parked fifty metres away spun around and roared off.

Mendez stood in silence beside Delany, his eyes squinting against the bright sunshine. A frown creased his forehead at the recognition of Leo Quinn glancing out the passenger window of the car in front as it spun around. 'Alonzo,' he said through gritted teeth.

'Boss, it's Mateo at the club,' said Arlo, holding the phone out to Mendez.

'Not now, Arlo. I don't want to hear about the club. You deal with it,' Mendez snapped back, his focus moving from the road to Gregory Delany as he tore strips off the men who had been standing outside the factory for not stopping the delivery truck.

'You're going to want to take this,' Arlo said calmly.

Mendez took the phone and put it to his ear. 'What is it, Mateo?'

'The Englishmen from last night, the same one and his friends. They hit the club. Ignore the shorts and stupid T-shirts, they're professionals. They took out the chef, then jumped me and Javier. We didn't have a chance. They were after the women. And boss?'

'What?'

'The fourth one who didn't join in last night or today, he has Mr Delany's memory stick.'

'You are sure?'

'Yes, boss, I heard them talking about it.'

Mendez's face darkened. He passed the phone back to Arlo without answering Mateo.

'Who the fuck are these guys?'

'I don't know, but I know how we can find out,' said Arlo, slipping the phone into his jacket.

'How?'

'The night manager from the Villa Venecia Hotel called this morning to say a group of English holidaymakers were asking about the disappearance of the women last night.'

'And you didn't think to mention this earlier?' Mendez said, shooting Arlo an angry look.

'I didn't see any point. We had the women, and it didn't seem that important,' Arlo said, his voice calm and features unaffected by Mendez's anger.

'Ok, get everyone together, and get us some fucking cars. If they are at the hotel, I want them.'

'If they're not there, the hotel will have photocopied their passports, so we can find out who they are,' Arlo said, getting back on his phone.

'And find out what Alonzo Acosta has got to do with

81

all this,' Mendez muttered.

'Samuel, what the fuck is going on?' Delany bellowed from behind him.

'I have cars on the way. Five minutes at the most,' Arlo said quietly into Mendez's ear.

'It's all under control, Gregory, cars are on the way. Those men have the women and the memory stick. But this is my town. They will not get far. This will be over soon,' Mendez said, turning to Delany.

'It fucking better be, Samuel. Whoever these clowns are, I want them dead. You understand me? Dead!' Delany shouted furiously.

CHAPTER 22

'Er, hi love,' Danny said over the noise of the truck.

'Hello future husband, how's the stag weekend going?' Nikki said, her voice all bubbly and bright.

'Er, yeah, it's definitely been a bit lively,' Danny said, shrugging to Scott as he tried to think of something to say while hanging on to the side of the truck as it went around another bend.

'You're not drunk already, are you? It's not even twelve yet. What's all that noise?' Nikki said, quizzing him.

'No, no, I haven't touched a drop yet. We're on an, er, open-top bus tour,' Danny said, the words not coming out as convincingly as he would have liked them to.

'Oh, ok, sounds like fun. Anyway, there's nothing to worry about, but your sister-in-law has gone into labour. Rob's up the hospital with her now.'

'Oh, for fuck's sake,' Danny said, looking out of the back of the truck at the black Mercedes that followed them from the club and Leo's car closing on them fast.

'I beg your pardon?' Nikki said, taken aback.

'What? Oh, sorry, love, no not you, er, I've got to go. Ferg's just got into an argument with the bus conductor. Great news about Tina. Let me know when it's born. Love you, bye, bye, bye,' Danny replied, talking quickly before hanging up and replacing the phone with the gun from the waistband of his shorts.

The passenger windows of the cars opened. Leo leaned out of the rear car, gun in hand. Daunte did the same out of the car directly behind them.

'Scott, tell Chaz and Fergus we've got company,' Danny yelled behind him.

'What? Oh crikey. Er, chaps, we've got a little problem back here,' shouted Scott, banging as hard as he could on the bulkhead to the driver's cab.

Hearing the thumps and Scott's muffled shouts, Chaz and Fergus simultaneously looked into the wing mirrors.

'Ferg!' Chaz said, passing him his gun.

'I'm on it,' Fergus replied, taking the gun in one hand and his own in the other. He twisted around in his seat and slid his top half out of the open window. Pointing both guns back down the side of the truck, Fergus tried to get a fix on the tyre of Chavez's car behind them. 'Hold it steady, Chaz,' Fergus shouted, his shots going wide when his aim moved up with the truck's bouncing.

'Everyone down,' Danny yelled, swinging behind a plastic wrapped pallet of ice cream containers a split second before Daunte opened fire, the bullets thudding into the frozen ice cream on the other side of the pallet, thankfully stopping somewhere in the middle of the stack, a couple of feet short of Danny. Moving to the side, Danny locked his arm up in front of him, looking down the sights of the gun at the centre of Daunte's forehead before gently squeezing the trigger. Much to his surprise, nothing happened. He moved back behind cover as Leo fired more bullets into the stack. Danny released the magazine, looking at it to confirm his worst fear. It wasn't loaded.

'Shit,' he said, tucking the empty gun into the back of his shorts.

Thinking fast, Danny reached up and pulled ice cream containers from the top of the pallet and ripped off their lids. He looked around the stack to see Leo's car brake and swerve in behind Chavez's as the road narrowed. Chavez lost his wing mirror in an explosion of plastic and glass when it caught a parked car, swerving to avoid Fergus's shots from the front of the truck. Taking aim, Danny launched one ice cream container after another. The heavy frozen blocks hit the windscreen and cracked the glass before bouncing off, leaving thick multi-coloured stripes of ice cream across the glass. Chavez jerked the steering wheel in surprise, flicking the windscreen wipers on and squirting the screen wash in a desperate attempt to see where he was going. His eyes went wide in terror when a section of screen cleared enough for him to see he'd gone off course and was metres away from a parked van. Chavez disappeared from view when the driver's airbag blew with the impact, the seatbelt snapping tight across his chest to bruise his ribs. Still hanging out of the window, the rapid deceleration and Daunte's momentum ripped him out of the crashed vehicle into the path of Leo's car close behind. Daunte bounced off the front of Leo's car like a broken rag doll. Without any concern for him, Tomás accelerated through the gap in pursuit of the truck.

'Scott, get over here and help me,' Danny yelled, before

crouching down to wedge his back into the wrapped stack of ice cream and pushing.

Scott jumped forward and did the same, the two of them pushing with all their might until the stack started to lean.

'That's it, just a bit more,' Danny grunted.

The resistance got less and less as they reached tipping point, the stack finally moving away from them before free-falling off the back of the truck. An almighty crash followed a split second later as it landed on the bonnet of Leo's car, crushing the suspension to the ground as it flattened the bonnet and crashed through the front windscreen. As they drove off into the distance, Danny and Scott stood looking out of the back of the truck to see Leo and Tomás kick the doors open and clamber out of the car covered in ice cream.

'I think it might be time to call it a day on the stag weekend,' said Danny.

'Yes, I think you might be right, old man. What do you suppose we do with the ladies and the memory stick?' said Scott, pulling it out of his pocket.

'I'll call our friend Edward Jenkins. I'm sure the Director of the Secret Intelligence Service will know the right person to deal with this. If that memory stick is important enough to warrant this amount of effort to get it back, the National Crime Agency and Border Force will be happy to take them into protective custody,' Danny said looking back at Louise and Sandra sitting huddled at the back of the lorry.

'Yes, that sounds like the most sensible option,' said Scott, slipping the memory stick back into his pocket.

'Let's get back to the hotel, check out, and get on the

next plane back home.' Danny made his way over scattered ice cream containers to the bulkhead and banged on it hard. 'Chaz, take us back to the hotel,' he yelled, sticking his ear against the cold surface to hear a muffled, 'Roger that,' coming back from Chaz.

CHAPTER 23

With steam coming out of the twisted front, the Helado de Frutas Mendez delivery truck limped up the hotel driveway before stopping directly outside of reception in a steaming mess with a frothy mixture of boiling coolant and oil dripping out onto the tarmac.

'Mind the paintwork, I've just had it waxed,' Chaz said, throwing the keys to the speechless valet.

He walked to the rear of the truck with Fergus and helped the ladies down to the ground.

'What are we doing here? This will be the first place they look. We've got to get out of here,' Louise said, a panicked look in her eyes.

'And we will, as soon as we get our stuff and passports. Look, I got yours from the club, here. Trust me, if you come back to the UK with us, I know people who will help you,' Danny said, trying to calm her down.

'The UK, no, no, we can't. We have to find a way of taking care of him here. If we go back to the UK he'll come after us, and you too. He has people everywhere,' Louise said hysterically.

'This is all your fault. What are we going to do now? You've put a target on our backs and you've dragged this lot into your mess as well. The only way to stop Gregory Delany is to kill him,' Sandra yelled at her sister, which spiralled the sisters into a full-blown argument.

Danny, Chaz, Fergus and Scott stood in a line behind them, hands in pockets, looking at each other, not knowing what to say while the sisters went at each other.

'Don't look at me, I'm with this twat,' Fergus mumbled, pointing at his T-shirt slogan and then at Chaz, which caused them both to snigger.

'Fergus, you smooth talker, fancy a shag?' Chaz replied, pointing at his T-shirt, which made them laugh harder and Danny chuckle.

'Oh, good grief, it's like looking after a bunch of three-year-olds. Right, sod the lot of you. I'm going to change out of my ruined shirt and pack,' Scott said, walking into the hotel.

The sisters' argument ran out of steam, leaving them all standing awkwardly in silence.

'Sorry, the last couple of days have been a lot. Thank you, all of you. I don't know what we would have done without you,' Louise finally said to them before turning to look at her sister.

'Yeah, that goes from me as well, thank you so much,' said Sandra, instantly forgiving her sister and hugging her.

'Don't mention it. Just cool it with the all the killing talk, ok? Come up with us while we get our stuff and we'll be out of here in no time,' said Danny, ushering them all towards the hotel entrance.

'You said you had people in the UK who can help us?' said Louise, managing a smile.

'Government people, people more powerful than your ex-boyfriend.'

'Who are you guys?' Sandra asked.

'Just four guys minding their own business on a stag weekend,' said Fergus, handing Chaz one of his handguns. Chaz took it and both of them tucked them into the back of their shorts before covering them with their pink T-shirts.

They crossed the reception, their eyes scanning every corner for anything out of character, Fergus and Chaz's right hands loose by their side, ready to pull the gun from the back of their shorts with a split second's notice. Watching Scott get into the lift ahead of him, Danny headed straight for the stairs, leading the rest of them up to their rooms on the third floor.

'Ok, no fucking about, five minutes, yeah. I want to be packed up and out of here.'

'Yes Staff,' Chaz and Fergus snapped back, their mood turning serious as they headed quickly to their rooms.

'You two can wait in my room while I pack,' Danny said, holding the hotel door open for them to enter.

Louise sat in the chair in the corner while Sandra sat on the corner of the bed next to her. Danny threw his small carry-on suitcase on the bed, gathering all his clothes and wash bag and dumping them all inside the case in thirty seconds flat. Catching his reflection in the mirror, he frowned and peeled the pink "The Stag," T-shirt off as the two sisters tried to look like they weren't looking at Danny's muscular torso covered in bullet, knife and shrapnel scars. After a quick spray of deodorant, he selected a more discreet T-shirt and put it on.

'Nearly ready,' he said, opening the cupboard with the

hotel safe inside. He rapidly punched the four-digit code that preceded the satisfying motorised sound of the locking bars withdrawing before the door popped open.

He grabbed his passport and money and shoved them into the pockets of his shorts.

'Right, let's go,' he said, moving around the bed to zip up his case. As he did so, he glanced out the window that overlooked the front of the hotel.

Five cars drove up the hotel drive at a speed that would suggest it wasn't guests arriving. He lost sight of them at the entrance to the hotel, the canopy at the front of the building obscuring his view.

'Shit, forget the case. We've got to go. Now.'

'What is it?' Sandra said, the worry returning to her face.

'Whatever happens, you do exactly as I say, ok?' Danny said, his face darkening as the muscles in his cheeks flexed and eyes narrowed.

'What? What do you mean, whatever happens?' Louise stuttered.

'Do exactly as I say and we will get you out of here. Do you understand?'

As the sisters nodded in silence, a series of knocks at the door, two, then three, then two, made them jump.

'It's ok, it's just the others.' Danny said, hurrying over to the door to open it.

'You see the cars?' Fergus said, with Chaz behind him.

'Yep, where's Scott?'

'Still in his room packing his ridiculously expensive shirts, I imagine. We thought we'd come here first.'

'Come on, let's go and get him. What's the ammo situation?' Danny asked, pulling the empty gun from behind him.

'I've got eight,' said Fergus.

'I've only got five,' said Chaz.

'Slide us three out, Ferg,' Danny asked, sliding the mag out.

'Here, take four,' Fergus said, pushing them out of his magazine and giving them to Danny, who loaded them and clicked the magazine back into the gun, pulling the slide back to chamber a round.

'Let's hope we don't need to use them,' said Danny, ushering the sisters out of the room.

'Roger that,' Chaz and Fergus said in unison, letting Danny lead the way up the corridor to Scott's room while they smiled and kept conversation light, keeping any sign of the nervousness they felt under wraps so they didn't freak the sisters out any more than they already were.

'Time to go, Scott,' Danny shouted, knocking repeatedly on Scott's door.

'Good grief, Daniel, I'm coming, where's the fire, old man?' Scott opened the door complaining, dressed back in his beige Ralph Lauren linen suit, his laptop bag over his shoulder while he wheeled his large Emporio Armani suitcase behind him.

'Leave that lot. We've gotta go. Now, Scotty boy,' Danny said, checking up and down the corridor nervously.

'What? Have you any idea how much this lot cost? I'm not leaving them,' Scott grumbled.

'You can't wear them if you're dead, mate. Now come on, we don't have time for this,' Danny said, fixing Scott with a look he didn't want to argue with.

'Very well, but I'm not leaving my laptop,' Scott said, pushing the suitcase back inside the room before closing the door.

'Fine, whatever, now let's get out of h—' Danny said, his answer cut short by the ding of the arriving lift a little way down the corridor.

Danny, Chaz and Fergus reacted with lightning speed, all moving like they were choreographed, turning side on to the corridor, while their right hands shot behind their backs to pull and snap their guns up and look along the sights at the opening lift doors. The cleaning trolley came out first, followed by one of the hotel maids, she took one look at the three guns pointed in her direction and screamed loudly. The three of them breathed out and dropped their guns.

'Scott, tell her we're not going to hurt her, and ask her if there's any other way out of here other than the lift or main stairs.'

Scott moved forward slowly, trying to pacify the maid and stop her crying. She eventually stopped and nodded when Scott pulled a hundred euros from his wallet and gave it to her. After saying something to him, she pointed to the far end of the corridor. Scott thanked her and returned to the others.

'She says there's a fire escape at the end of the corridor.'

'Lets go. Scott, you stay in the middle with the ladies, Chaz on me, Ferg, cover the rear.'

'Roger that,' Ferg said, moving fast while facing backwards, while the rest of them ran to the fire escape.

CHAPTER 24

Delany and Mendez got out of the lead vehicle with Arlo and Mateo, they headed past the valet who was still trying to figure out what he was supposed to do with the Helado de Frutas Mendez delivery truck. Sixteen men from the other four cars followed, looking like they were going to a convention for criminals, all wearing jackets to conceal a multitude of weapons underneath. Delany headed straight to the reception desk with no regard for the guests, who moved away apprehensively at the sight of a collection of hard, unfriendly men you wouldn't want to meet in a dark alley close behind him.

'Fuck off. Now,' Delany growled, interrupting the guest, talking to the manager.

'Excuse me, I'm talking,' the man said before Arlo put a massive hand on his shoulder and looked menacingly down at him.

'You heard the man. Fuck off,' he said calmly.

As he scooted off, the manager went white as a sheet at the sight of Delany, Mendez, Mateo and Arlo glaring at him from the other side of the reception desk, with sixteen thugs standing a couple of metres behind them.

'C-can I-I help you, sir?' he stammered out.

'Four men and two women got out of the delivery truck out front. Who are they and where did they go?' Delany said, leaning over the desk at the manager who leant back away from him.

'I, I'm sorry, sir, I didn't see them arrive. And I can't give you information about our guests. Client confidentiality, I'm afraid.' He replied, beads of sweat trickling down from his temple.

'You should be,' Delany said, looking up at a camera on the wall behind the reception. 'This hotel has cameras throughout?'

'Yes, sir.'

'Where are the monitors?' Delany said, the intensity of his stare making the manager physically squirm.

'They're in my office, but I can't let you see them.'

'Through there?' Delany pointed to a door at the far end of the reception.

'Well, yes but, I, what are you doing?' he said, panicking as Delany walked around the reception desk toward him with Mendez, Mateo and Arlo close behind. Delany shot a hand out and grabbed the manager's tie, pulling it down hard to drag the hunched over manager into his own office. The terrified receptionist lifted the phone to call the police. As she got it to her ear, one of Mendez's men stepped forward and shook his head, his hand moving his jacket to one side to flash a Glock 17 in a shoulder holster. Shaking, the woman slowly lowered the phone receiver and stood where she was, trying not to cry.

'Where the fuck are they?' Delany said impatiently, looking across all the camera feeds.

'Rewind the reception camera,' Mendez ordered the manager.

'I, I'm not supposed to.'

'Do it!' Delany shouted, pulling his gun and pushing the muzzle into the manager's sweaty temple.

'Stop. There, forward a bit,' Mendez said until there was a clear image of Danny and the others crossing the reception to the stairs.

'Mateo, which one of them is the boss?' Mendez said.

'The tall one, him. The one with "The Stag" T-shirt on,' Mateo said, tapping the monitor on the image of Danny.

'Follow them, the floor cameras, rewind them. Now,' Delany growled, pushing the gun even harder into the terrified man's temple.

'Ok, ok, please don't hurt me.'

'Shut up and do it.'

They watched the feeds whizzing back on all the floors until they caught sight of Danny and the others grouped in the corridor as a maid stepped out of the lift with her cleaning cart.

'Stop, that one. Rewind it. Where is that?'

'That's the third floor,' the manager said as the recording played the confrontation with the maid, followed by the group heading away from the camera to the far end of the corridor.

'Where are they going?'

'The rear stairwell. There's a fire exit door at the end of the corridor. It leads to a stairwell.'

'Where does it come out? Quickly tell me.'

'It goes all the way down past the kitchens on the lower level to the underground car park in the basement.'

'How do we get to it?'

'The fire escape door in the corner of reception,' said

the manager, tears coming from his eyes and snot dribbling from his nose.

'Arlo, take the men and find them, quickly,' Delany shouted, before turning his attention back to the manager. 'You take copies of the guests' passports when they arrive, yes?'

'Yes, it's the law. We have to keep a register of the guest's details.'

'Get me his,' Delany said, taking the gun away from the manager's head to point at the image of Danny.

In shock and racked with fear, the manager stayed in his seat.

'Don't just sit there. Move it. Hurry up and you might just live to see tomorrow.'

CHAPTER 25

'Shall we go for a hard and fast exit across reception?' Chaz said, his hand gripping the door on the ground floor that led that way.

'No, five cars, Chaz. There'll be too many of them. Let's go down and cut through the restaurant. With a bit of luck we can slip out amongst the guests and head past the pool and gardens without being noticed,' Danny said, continuing down the stairs to the LG level.

He opened the door a crack to look into a service corridor outside, closing it quickly when he heard trolley wheels clattering along the tiled floor from the opposite direction. After a few seconds Danny opened the door again to see a member of the kitchen staff disappear out of sight, pushing a trolley full of dirty dishes into the kitchen through the closing doors opposite the stairwell. Opening the door wider, Danny stuck his head out and looked in the direction the trolley had come from, relieved to see the restaurant was only a few metres away.

'Let's go, stay close,' said Danny, slipping out the door. Chaz held it open while he ushered Scott and the sisters out, Fergus went next, his head swinging from one end of the corridor to the other before following the others, safe in the knowledge that Chaz had his back. Danny stopped short of the end of the corridor, his hand up behind him to stop the others as he flattened himself against the wall. He moved his head out just far enough for one eye to see into the restaurant, spinning back into the corridor after spotting a bunch of Mendez's men heading in their direction.

'Back to the stairs, go, go, go,' he whispered.

Chaz and Fergus reacted before Danny had finished speaking. Chaz held the door open again while Fergus and Danny hustled the others into the stairwell. As the door shut behind them, sound echoed down from the reception door opening as many pairs of feet came down the stairs towards them.

'Go, go, down the stairs,' Danny shouted, pulling his gun out and emptying all four rounds up the stairwell. The sound was deafening in the confined space. The second the gun clicked empty, Danny slid the magazine out and pushed the end under the door to the kitchen and restaurant. Tossing the gun as he stood and kicked the magazine, jamming it under the door. As he turned to head after the others, a deafening volley of return fire came from above, bullets sparked and pinged as they ricocheted all around him. Danny leaped down the stairs, clearing the steps to plant his feet solidly on the landing below. His shoulder hit the wall hard before he bounced off and leaped down the next set of steps, flying through the door to the underground car park held open by Chaz.

'Car?' Danny said, as Chaz pushed the door shut.

'Ferg's on it.'

'Gun,' Danny ordered.

Chaz handed it over without a word. He knew they didn't have time to discuss the whys and why nots. Danny took it and ran over to a couple just about to get into a small rental car.

'Keys, now,' he ordered, pointing his gun at the man about to get into the driver's seat.

He handed them over with a shaking hand, backing off as Danny jumped in and started the engine. The second it fired, he jammed it into reverse and hurtled backwards out of the parking space. Looking back over his shoulder, Danny yanked the steering wheel and squealed the tyres as he turned on the smooth concrete. Still driving backwards, Danny lined the car up with the door to the stairwell and put his foot down. One of Mendez's men opened the door, with several more men directly behind him. As he peered into the underground car park his eyes went wide at the sight of the little car hurtling backwards towards him, its rear hitting the door before he could get clear. The force of the impact smashed the door into his body, launching him backwards, knocking everyone behind him over like a strike at a bowling alley. The car continued until it hit the wall on either side of the door with an almighty boom that echoed across the underground car park. Pushing the exploded airbag out the way, Danny yanked on the handbrake and jumped out of the car and joined Chaz.

'That should keep them busy for a while.'

The screech of tyres and beams from headlights on their backs cast their shadows over the wrecked hire car. They spun around. Chaz snapped his gun up as he turned, his aim pointing beyond the blinding lights to the position where the driver sat. As his finger tensed on the trigger, a shadowy outline of a head stuck itself out of the driver's window.

'Oi! You couple of tarts going to get in, or are you going to spend all day exchanging insurance details?' came Fergus's voice from the shadows.

'Fuck, thanks for scaring the shit out of us, Ferg,' said Chaz, walking around the front of the car.

'You're welcome, mate. Oh, you'll have to get in the boot, the back's full.'

'Terrific, this day just gets better and better,' grumbled Chaz, walking to the back of the Mercedes SUV, lifting the hatchback up to see a young guy cowering in the back. 'Who the fuck is this?'

'Ah yeah, that's the parking valet. He was kind enough to give me the car keys. Chuck him out while you're back there, Chaz.'

Danny climbed into the front passenger seat. 'You guys alright?' he said, turning back in his seat to look at Sandra, Louise and Scott, still clutching his laptop bag, while Chaz threw the young valet out of the boot and climbed in, pulling the door down to shut it behind him.

'Tip top, my dear fellow. Any chance we could get out of here?' Scott said sarcastically while the sisters just nodded at Danny.

'Here we go,' Fergus said, looking back over his shoulder as he launched the car in reverse, the gearbox screaming until he found a space big enough to manoeuvre. Locking the brakes up, Fergus spun the steering wheel hard, sliding the car through a one-eighty before jamming it into first gear and hitting the accelerator. The car shot out of the underground car park and squealed up the ramp. By the time he reached the exit on one side of the hotel's main entrance, the car was going so fast the wheels left the ground. They thumped back down on the drive, causing the car to snake until Fergus got it under control and accelerated away from the hotel.

'We good, Chaz?' Danny shouted, ducking his head as he tried to see the hotel foyer behind them.

'Yeah, we're clear, no one's following,' Chaz replied, his eyes glued to the front of the hotel through the rear window.

'Let's go to the airport. We'll be safe there. And slow it down, Ferg, we don't want to get arrested on the way there.'

'Roger that,' Fergus said, checking the mirror and easing the speed down through the Benidorm streets, heading towards the main road to Alicante and the airport.

With no one following, the group relaxed a little. The sunshine cut between the bars and restaurants and side roads, putting them in a better mood. Up ahead, they could see the junction to the main road out of town getting closer.

The first they knew about the collision was the almighty boom and sideways shunt. The windows imploded, showering them in glass crystals as the Land Rover continued to push Danny and the others sideways until the other side of the car crunched into the front of a restaurant, making it impossible to open the nearside doors. Disorientated, Danny looked out the glassless window at the Land Rover embedded into the wing and front passenger door. Men and cars poured out of the side road behind the Land Rover, and a dozen guns instantly pointing in their direction. Leo walked between them and opened the back door. 'You've got to the count of three to tell me where the memory stick is,' he said, grabbing

Sandra and pulling her out of the car to put a gun to her head.

'One. Two.'

Danny and Fergus sat helplessly trapped in the front of the car, while Chaz sat in the boot staring at four guns pointed at his head.

'Wait, don't hurt her. I've got it,' Scott said, patting his laptop case as he eased out of the car slowly.

'You as well, out,' Leo said to Louise, while Tomás and Chavez bundled Sandra and Scott into a waiting car.

As soon as Louise was out, Leo pushed her into the back after Scott and Sandra, slamming the door on them. He immediately got into the front and the car sped away as the door was closing. The rest of the men backed away slowly, climbing into the other vehicles before they tore off after Leo, leaving Danny, Fergus, and Chaz stuck in the car.

'Fuck, fuck, fucking fuckers, now I'm really pissed off,' Danny shouted, bringing both feet up to stamp them repeatedly on the inside of the front windscreen until it gave way, flopping out onto the bonnet. He climbed out with Fergus, then walked around the Land Rover buried into the side of the Mercedes to let Chaz out of the boot.

The three of them stood in the street looking in the direction the cars had gone.

'We should get out of here,' Chaz said, looking at a small crowd of people slowly appearing to see what was going on.

Danny looked into the Land Rover. The keys were in the ignition and the engine was still running. He jumped in and stuck it in reverse, revved it up and eased the clutch up. A metallic screech mixed with the sound of plastic snapping rang out until the Land Rover detached itself from the side of the Mercedes and jumped back a few feet.

'Get in,' Danny shouted out the window.

As soon as Fergus and Chaz shut the doors, Danny floored it and sped off, bits of headlight and bumper falling off as he went.

'Great, so what the fuck do we do now?' Chaz said from the back seat.

'They weren't Mendez's men. It was the same guys who were watching the club this morning and then waiting for us outside the factory earlier. They have to be Delany or Mendez's competition.'

'Right, so how do we find out who they are?' said Fergus.

'We go and see the man the memory stick belongs to,' said Danny, his face dark and menacing.

'Er, run that by me again,' said Chaz.

CHAPTER 26

High up in the hills of Maylan, Leo drove through the electric gates of Alonzo Acosta's villa, followed by the rest of Alonzo's men. They pulled up next to a collection of other cars already parked on the large drive. Armed men in dark suits and shades stood in various positions around the outside of the villa and around the gardens and gate. Leo and Chavez hustled Scott, Louise, and Sandra out of the vehicle and marched them around to the pool terrace. He lined them up at one end of a large glass-topped table. Alonzo Acosta sat cross-legged and relaxed in an expensive linen suit at the other end.

'Which one has the memory stick?' he said in Spanish to Leo, as if they didn't exist.

'That one,' Leo said, pointing his gun towards Scott with his laptop bag over his shoulder.

'The memory stick, please,' Alonzo said, flipping into perfect English with a smile.

With Leo and Chavez's guns still pointed at his head, Scott reluctantly pulled the memory stick out of the zip up pocket on the front of the laptop bag and handed it to Chavez, who eagerly took it to Alonzo.

'You see, that wasn't difficult, was it? Now, which one of you two ladies is Mr Delany's girlfriend? Ah, that would be you, blondie,' he said, watching the fear spread across Louise's face at the mention of Delany's name. 'Now I wonder what kind of deal Gregory Delany will be prepared to do to get this and you back. Maybe he'll cut Mendez out of the picture and put me in charge of distribution,' Alonzo said, twiddling the memory stick around in his fingers.

He sat staring at the three of them for a while before speaking. 'Kill the other two. They are of no use to me,' he ordered, looking at Chavez.

Without hesitation, Chavez levelled his gun at Scott's temple and started to squeeze the trigger.

'Not here, you idiot. You and Tomás take them to the marina. Use my boat and drop them out at sea, use plenty of weight. I don't want them washing ashore. Dead tourists are bad for business.'

'Yes sir,' Chavez said, grabbing Scott by the arm.

'Wait, no, hang on. Don't you want to know what's on it?' Scott blurted out as Chavez and Tomás manhandled him and Sandra towards the cars.

'Wait, bring them back,' Alonzo ordered, waiting until they were lined up again before he continued. 'It's encrypted. You can't access it.'

'I can,' Scott said confidently.

'And why should I believe you, Mr …?'

'Miller, Scott Miller of Miller Computer Systems Ltd.'

'Shit, I knew I'd seen him somewhere. He's the guy, the guy who stopped that cyber terrorist who tried to crash the banks,' Tomás said, switching to Spanish as he spoke to Alonzo.

Alonzo looked at the memory stick, thinking about the secrets it held, then looked back at Scott.

'What do you need to get into it?'

'Just my laptop. Some time, and the promise you will let all of us go once I've done it,' Scott said, holding his stare with Alonzo's.

Alonzo didn't move for an uncomfortably long time.

'Done. Take them inside and give Mr Miller whatever he needs,' Alonzo said, getting up to hand the memory stick back to Scott.

'Oh, and Leo, kill the Wi-Fi. I don't want Mr Miller getting any funny ideas about contacting the authorities.'

'Yes boss,' Leo replied.

They were just about to step inside when Alonzo called after them. 'Mr Miller.'

Scott stopped and turned to look at him.

'Do not try to fool me. There are more painful ways to die than drowning,' he said, sitting back in his chair before waving his hand to dismiss them.

They took Scott and the sisters to a lounge area to one side of the kitchen and sat them down. Leo disappeared, leaving Tomás and Chavez to sit at the breakfast bar where they could keep an eye on them.

'Can you really get into the memory stick?' Louise whispered to Scott.

'Undoubtedly, my dear. But I rather fear that if I do, they will kill us anyway. Have faith, I'm just trying to buy us time until Daniel and the others find us,' Scott said, giving her a reassuring smile, which dropped the second Leo returned to the room.

'How long is this going to take?' he said gruffly.

'My dear fellow, this is a 256-bit AES encryption, military-grade USB memory stick. It's going to take a good few hours at least to break through the security encryption. How about a nice glass of iced water? It would do wonders for my concentration,' said Scott while opening his laptop.

Leo glared at him before walking off. 'Get him what he wants,' he growled at Chavez before storming out of the room.

'Thank you. What about the ladies?' Scott said, when Chavez returned with his drink.

Chavez turned and headed back into the kitchen, barely hiding his annoyance.

Scott plugged the memory stick into his laptop and instantly started opening windows and programmes before entering row after row of code as he typed furiously on the keys.

CHAPTER 27

Danny drove slowly past Club Desire, parking tightly behind a delivery van so prying eyes wouldn't notice the damage to the front of the vehicle. All three of them twisted around in their seats to look back down the road at the club. The restaurant opposite was filling up with holidaymakers, mostly families taking their children out for an early evening meal before Benidorm centre turned into party time with stag and hen parties and the usual pissed-up holidaymakers.

'You sure you want to do this? There are a lot of civilians about,' Chaz said, worried about the kids in the restaurant.

'You guys don't have to come if you don't want to,' Danny said, seeing the neon lights come on as the club opened for business.

'Piss off,' said Chaz, annoyed that Danny even thought something like that, let alone said it..

'Yeah, shut up, you twat, or I'll kill you myself,' added Fergus.

'Ok, ok, I'll shut up. Right, plan of attack?' Danny said

to the two men, who were more like brothers to him than friends.

'I'm voting for front door, shock and awe tactics. Hit them hard and get upstairs to the boss man before we get our brains blown out,' said Fergus.

The other two looked at each other, shrugged, then nodded.

'That's the plan sorted. I'll go in first and take out the doorman. I doubt he'll be armed. They wouldn't want the punters to see guns. But with all that's been going on, I bet there'll be someone close by who has got a weapon. While they focus on me, you two disarm whoever that might be, ok?' Danny said.

'Roger that,' Chaz and Fergus replied in unison.

'After that, we move through the public area at the front and go straight for the stairs to the office. We need to get from the entrance door to the office as fast as possible. We don't want them alerted that we're coming,' said Danny, mentally walking himself through the club and up the stairs to the office.

'What do you reckon, Ferg, inside of sixty seconds?'

'I reckon that'll be about right, Chaz, me old mate.'

'Right, let's do this,' Danny said, getting out of the vehicle.

The other followed as Danny went to the boot of the Land Rover and opened it up. He lifted the panel in the boot and pulled out the wheel nut wrench from the tool kit underneath. Slamming the boot shut, he turned and walked towards the club entrance with Chaz and Fergus on each side.

'Ready?'

'Yep,' said Chaz.

'Roger that. See you on the other side, boys,' said

Fergus before the three of them walked casually towards the entrance.

Fergus and Chaz hung back a little to give Danny a couple of seconds' lead.

Danny turned into the entrance with the tyre wrench held behind his back. Two suited bouncers stood on either side of the ticket booth and cloakroom, eyeing the punters up and down as they paid the entry fee. The second he was through the door, Danny had taken in the bouncers, the women behind the counter and an armed man standing by the coats in the cloakroom behind her. Under the misconception that nothing could possibly happen at the club, the armed man was relaxed, and looked more interested in checking out the cashier's tits as he peered down her low cut top than he was about the people who entered the club.

Moving right as he stepped forward, Danny went low, bringing the tyre iron out to swing hard, striking the side of the bouncer's knee joint. The big man went down, his knee joint giving way before the pain had time to register in his brain. Watching the other bouncer turning in his direction as if he was moving in slow motion, Danny whipped the tyre iron up, putting all his body weight behind it as he cracked the second man on the temple. While Danny watched the guy go down like a felled tree, Fergus rushed past behind him, hurdling the cashier's desk with his gun out in front. It was in the face of the armed man before he had a chance to pull his eyes out of the cashier's cleavage.

'Evening,' Fergus said, sliding his free hand inside the guy's jacket to remove his gun and toss it behind him, over the cashier, to Danny.

Danny caught it while Chaz shut the entrance doors to

the club and slid the bolt to lock them. Leaping over the desk, Danny grabbed some empty wire hangers off the coat rail and twisted them apart before pulling the man's arms behind his back. He wound the hanger wire around the wrists before pushing the man to the ground to wind another hanger around his ankles.

'That's it. Let's go, go, go,' Danny said, ripping the cable from the phone on the cashier's desk out of the wall so she couldn't call the office. Jumping back over the desk the three of them entered the club.

CHAPTER 28

'I don't care if you've finished work for the day. You fucking go back and find out who these men are, where they live and who they work for,.' Delany shouted down the phone as he studied the photocopy of Danny's passport he'd just sent to DCI Matthew Cain.

His face went bright red, contorting in anger at the silence coming back at him.

'Cain,' he yelled.

'I'm here,' Cain finally said.

'Do what I pay you for. You hear me, Cain?'

'Yes, Mr Delany,' came Cain's resigned voice.

He hung up, still staring at the picture of Danny, studying every little detail in the little passport photo before folding it up and sliding it into his jacket pocket.

'Where the fuck are they? You told me you had this town covered.'

'We'll find them. I've got people out everywhere looking for them and I've got Arlo covering the airport. They haven't been anywhere near it.'

A knock at the door stopped Delany from tearing another strip off Mendez.

'What?' Delany yelled, the words barely leaving his mouth before the door burst open with the force of Javier flying backwards through it.

Danny stepped through in his wake, moving to one side to let Chaz and Fergus move in beside him. All three of them fanned out, covering Delany, Mendez and two of their men with their guns.

'Weapons out slowly. Between the fingers and place them on the floor, then kick them over to me,' Danny said, his eyes locked on Delany's, neither of them relinquishing command of the situation by looking away.

The tension in the room grew. Seconds felt like minutes until the men moved slowly, pulling their guns out by the butt to place them on the floor before kicking them in Danny's direction.

'So what happens next, eh? What, you here to kill me? Go on then, fucking kill me. You'll be dead before the night's out,' Delany said defiantly before adding, 'Who do you work for, Balentine? Acosta? Greco? Whatever they're paying you, I can double it.'

'We don't give a fuck about you or your business, you stupid bastard. Now shut up and listen. I'll get you your memory stick, ok? But in return, you forget you've ever seen us or Sandra and Louise Benning,' Danny said, cutting Delany dead.

There was another painful silence until Delany spoke.

'What do you mean, get the memory stick? I thought you had it?' he said in a low, calm voice.

'A black Mercedes followed us from the factory. Spanish guy, mid-forties, slicked-back grey hair. Who is he?' Danny said, ignoring Delany's question.

'Leo Quinn, he's Alonzo Acosta's right-hand man,' Mendez said.

'He ambushed us and has the memory stick along with my friend and the Benning sisters. If you agree to leave us all alone, I'll get it back for you.'

Delany continued to look into Danny's eyes. No matter how long he stared, he saw no weakness in the man in front of him.

'Get me the memory stick and you're free to go,' he said, leaning back into the leather office chair.

'And your ex?' Danny said, pressing the point.

Delany smiled before answering.

'Yes, and Louise.'

'Ok, tell me where I can find Alonzo Acosta,' Danny said, picking up the gun by his foot and tucking it into his waistband.

CHAPTER 29

The room shrank around Scott, his concentration so deep it gave him tunnel vision on the code streaming down the laptop screen. His fingers had been dancing over the keys for a couple of hours now and he was making steady progress through the layers of encryption.

'Ah, there you are,' he whispered.

After typing in a command, Scott's fingers ceased to move across the keyboard. After hours of rhythmic tapping, the sudden silence made Louise and Sandra look over. Scott caught the movement of their heads out of the corner of his eye and turned to look in their direction. Worried that Chavez might have noticed as well, Scott looked into the kitchen, relieved to see Chavez still sitting on the stool by the breakfast bar, his eyes glued to his phone as he flicked around on social media, bored. Scott turned his attention back to the sisters and held a finger to his lips before returning to the laptop and hitting the enter key. The code disappeared and a large window opened, displaying all the folders stored on the memory stick. Scott took a quick glance over at Chavez to make sure he was still engrossed on his phone, which he was. Looking back at his laptop, Scott started opening folders and flicking through their contents.

'My, my, no wonder you want to get your grubby little fingers on this,' he said to himself in a whisper.

Scott checked the Wi-Fi on the laptop again, just in case it was on or he could piggyback off somebody else's nearby. He frowned when none was available.

If I can't send the contents to the authorities and I can't call for help, what is one to do?

He sat deep in thought for a while before an idea came into his head and a smile spread across his face. Seconds later, he opened another window and started tapping away at the keys, typing line after line of incomprehensible code into an open window. Over at the breakfast bar, Chavez looked up from his phone. Something about the way Louise glanced his way, then nervously looked back at Scott, piqued his interest.

'Scott,' Louise whispered as Chavez stood up off his stool.

Scott didn't react. His already fast moving fingers sped up to almost a blur. Out of the corner of his eye, he could see Chavez moving in his direction.

Come on, come on, nearly there.

Chavez paused when he reached the sofa where Sandra and Louise sat side by side. He looked down at them as they avoided his gaze before looking across at Scott, working away. He moved towards him, circling around the back of the sofa Scott sat on so he could see what was on the laptop screen in front of him. As the glowing screen came into view, Scott's fingers abruptly stopped before his index finger punched the enter key, all the open windows vanished from the screen. All that was left was a blank desktop screen with one small open window streaming continual lines of code from left to right.

'What were you just doing?' Chavez said, frowning.

'My dear fellow, I spent years at university and an entire career learning how to do what I do. I could explain it to you, but do you really think you'd understand it?' Scott said with a certain amount of smugness.

'Just hurry up and get into that memory stick,' Chavez said angrily, turning away from Scott.

'I'll have another iced water if you don't mind,' Scott said, unable to resist the opportunity to push Chavez's buttons.

He stopped midway to the kitchen, his fist clenching until his knuckles went white. For a second Scott thought he might have pushed Chavez a little too far, but after a second or two he unclenched his fist and continued into the kitchen. He fetched Scott his drink and brought it over, thumping it down hard on the coffee table, making it spill onto the glass surface.

'Drink your drink, Englishman, if you don't hurry up and get into that memory stick, it will be the last one you have,' he said, returning to his kitchen stool to scroll through more social media videos on his phone.

Scott looked away from Chavez to the frightened sisters on the other sofa. 'Don't worry, it will all be alright,' he said, giving them the most reassuring smile he could.

CHAPTER 30

Flipping the sun visor down, Danny squinted against the sinking sun as they drove up into the hills and the town of Maylan. They continued upwards towards the address on the edge of town that Mendez had given them. As they got closer, Danny spotted two men sitting in a car by the side of the road. Their body language, sunglasses and the prison tattoos on the back of the driver's hand as it hung out the window, gave them away.

'Eyes on,' Danny said.

'Yeah, I see them,' said Chaz, taking a quick right turn to take them away from their destination before they alerted Alonzo Acosta's men.

He pulled up a little way further on and turned the engine off. The three of them sat in silence for a few moments, watching the sun sink behind the hills beyond Maylan.

'Ready?'

'Yep,' replied Chaz.

'Let's go and get the posh twat. If anyone's going to kill him, it's gonna be me,' said Fergus from the back.

The three of them stepped out of the vehicle and pulled up the top half of the black boiler suits they'd bought at a builders' merchant in Benidorm. Moving around the back of the vehicle, they took a quick look around before opening the boot. They slipped on black baseball caps with a picture of a wrench and the name of a well known Spanish tool manufacturer, Irega, above it. After pulling on black latex gloves, Fergus put a roll of gaffer tape in his pocket before dividing a bag of zip ties up and handing them out to Danny and Chaz.

'Here,' Danny said, twisting the lid off a tin of black boot polish before passing it over to Fergus.

'Thanks, this is the only way I'm going to get a bit of colour on this bloody holiday,' he chuckled, wiping his fingers over the waxy substance before rubbing it evenly on his face.

'You're right about that one,' Chaz said, doing the same.

The two of them finished and gave each other a big grin, the whites of their teeth standing out in the darkening sky.

'Ok, let's tool up,' Danny said, flipping the blanket in the back to one side to expose an array of Glock 17 handguns, shoulder holsters and three pump-action shotguns, all courtesy of Samuel Mendez.

'Everyone clear on the plan?' Danny asked.

'Yep, cut through a neighbouring property, circle around to the rear of the property, then work our way through the trees and bushes until we reach the back of Acosta's villa,' said Chaz.

'Once there, we hop over the wall and make a break for the house,' Fergus added.

'We need to locate Scott and the sisters without raising the alarm. If it turns into a shit-shoot before we get inside, then the chances of getting them out alive are slim to none,' Danny said, sliding the last cartridge into the shotgun.

'Roger that,' said Chaz, while Fergus nodded his agreement.

'But before that, we need to deal with the chuckle brothers on lookout,' Danny said, shutting the boot down.

'Well, what are we waiting for?' grinned Chaz.

'Ah, just like old times,' added Fergus.

The three of them moved back down the road, staying in the shadows as they hugged the outside walls and gates all the way to the corner. Danny swung his head around and looked over the top of the parked cars on his side of the road at the lookout car opposite. He could see the outline of the two men sitting in the car in the dark. Two red dots glowed from inside the car, followed by puffs of smoke drifting out the open windows as they exhaled cigarette smoke. The flicker from the headlights of an approaching car made Danny and the others duck down behind the parked car beside them. They watched through the windows as the headlights lit up the faces of the two men in the lookout car, both of them holding a hand up to shield their eyes from the blinding light.

'Let's move,' Danny said, crouching low under the cover of the parked cars as he headed up the road.

He stopped when he'd gone beyond the rear of the lookout car, tucking down behind a small white van while the approaching car stopped level with the lookout car. The men inside talked to each other in a flurry of Spanish before the car drove on, its headlights fading away, leaving the lookout car in the dark once more. While the occupants' eyes were still adjusting to the dark after being dazzled by the bright headlights, Danny, Chaz and Fergus scooted across the road and bobbed down behind the rear of their car. Danny placed his shotgun gently on the tarmac and pulled out a handgun. After Chaz and Fergus did the same, he pointed for Chaz to go around the far side of the car and for Fergus to get in the back. As they nodded their agreement, Danny counted his fingers down from three to one. When he got to none, he and Chaz spun around to each side of the car in perfect synchronicity. They took two steps forward, sliding their Glocks in through the open windows to place the barrels onto the temples of the unsuspecting occupants.

'You speak English?' Danny said.

'Yes,' the driver answered.

While this was going on, Fergus pulled the back door open and slid into the seat behind them. He leaned forward between the two front seats and relieved the men of their guns before patting their jacket pockets until he found their phones.

'How many men are at the villa?' Danny said, pushing the gun against the temple a little harder as he asked.

'I don't know, ten, maybe twelve,' the driver answered, the scared look on his face making Danny believe him.

'How are they spread out?'

'I, er, I …'

'Tell me,' Danny growled, pulling the slide back on top of the Glock to instil more fear into the driver.

'F-f-five patrolling the garden, two on the gate, maybe three inside with Quinn and Acosta.'

'Where is our friend and the women?'

'They are at the back of the villa in the lounge by the kitchen,' the driver answered while shaking with fear.

'Shit, five's a lot to get past without being seen,' Chaz said from the other side of the car.

'I know, we're going to need a diversion of some sort,' Danny replied, moving the gun away from the driver's temple a few inches before nodding to Fergus in the back.

Before he knew what was happening, a loop made of zip ties went over the driver's head and the headrest before being pulled tight until it dug into his neck. Fergus didn't stop until the back of the driver's head was pinned to the leather headrest, the tight plastic tie making it difficult, but not impossible, for him to breathe. As he gasped for air, Fergus pulled his hands around the back of the seat and zip tied his wrists tightly together. Sliding across the back seat, Fergus restrained the guy sitting in the passenger seat in the same way. Reaching into his pocket, Fergus finished off by slapping a piece of gaffer tape across his mouth before tearing a second piece off to gag the driver.

'No, wait,' Danny said, stopping Fergus.

'You, if you see anyone, who are you supposed to call?' Danny said, moving the gun back to the driver's temple.

'Leo, we call Leo,' he gasped.

'Pass us his phone, Ferg.'

'Here,' Fergus said, reaching between the seats.

Danny held it up to the driver's face to unlock it, then moved through the menu to disable the facial and fingerprint locks.

'Hang on,' Danny said, stopping Fergus from gagging the driver a second time.

'For fuck's sake, what now? We're going to be here all night,' Fergus grumbled.

'What's the Spanish word for help?' he asked the driver.

'Fuck you, I've said enough. You're not going to kill me. You would have done it already,' he hissed back.

'Maybe not, but I've got no problem with blowing your dick off. Spanish for help, three, two, one,' Danny said, moving his face millimetres away from the driver's face while shoving the barrel of his gun into the driver's crotch.

'*Ayuda*, it's *ayuda*. Fuck. Mm, mmmn,' he said, the sentence cut short by Fergus slapping the strip of gaffer tape over his mouth.

'Let's go,' Danny said, pulling the keys out of the ignition and standing back out of the car to slam the door.

He hurled the keys into a hedge and joined the others around the back of the car. They picked up the shotguns and immediately disappeared through the gardens of the nearest villa with no lights on.

CHAPTER 31

Delany had been pacing around Mendez's office like a bear with a sore head for hours. Mendez sat at his desk with Arlo perched on the corner. They watched Delany silently, reluctant to speak and invoke his anger.

'It's been three hours. What the fuck is going on?' he shouted, not directed at anyone in particular.

'You should have let me deal with Acosta instead of this bunch of British clowns,' Arlo grumbled to Mendez in Spanish.

Delany heard Arlo's comments and understood every word. He whipped his head around with a furious look on his face.

'You! These British clowns have been running rings around you for two days, you fucking idiot. One more word out of you and I'll shoot you myself,' Delany yelled, his phone ringing with DCI Cain's ID showing, saving Arlo from a further ear bashing.

'Talk to me,' he ordered down the phone.

'I got the information on this guy Danny Pearson.'

'Well, go on then,' Delany said, his voice rising with his impatience.

'You're not going to like it. This guy's got more access denied and restricted files than I've ever seen before. He's like some goddamned national hero. If I try to dig further, I'll have the police commissioner and National Security on my arse asking why I want to know. I'll send you all I have, but if you want my advice, whatever you're thinking of doing, don't. You mess with this guy and you're going to have a bunch of men in black suits knocking on your front door within the hour.'

'Understood,' Delany said. Hanging up, he looked at Mendez and Arlo while he processed what Cain had said.

His phone buzzed a second later with Danny's file from Cain. Delany took his eyes off Mendez and Arlo while he scrolled through the information that wasn't either redacted in blacked out print or stamped *Restricted Access.*

'When they come back with the memory stick, we let them go,' he finally said, his voice unusually subdued.

'You're sure? After they left, you were going to kill them and take your woman back home with you,' Mendez said, puzzled at the sudden change of plan.

'Do not question my decision,' Delany snapped back before slumping into a chair.

'What if they don't come back?' Arlo piped up.

Delany's face hardened again as his attention turned back to Arlo.

'If they're not back by dawn, you get your chance to redeem yourself. You kill Acosta and every one of his men.'

The giant of a man just nodded his approval and the room dropped back into an uneasy silence, all three men watching the seconds tick away on the office clock.

CHAPTER 32

'Ready,' Danny said, the three of them standing far enough up the hill that they could look down over Acosta's property wall at his gardens and the rear of the building.

'Who's doing which bit?' Chaz said.

'I'll play the driver. *Ayunda, ayunda, rapido,*' Fergus said in his best distressed voice.

'A Scottish Spaniard, really Ferg?' Danny said, shaking his head.

'What? I thought I was good,' Fergus grumbled.

'*Ayunda, ayunda, rapido,*' Chaz said in a much more convincing Spanish accent.

'Good, you do some shouts and grunts with a few smacking sounds. I'll hold the phone over there so it sounds faint,' Danny said, moving a few metres away.

He looked at Chaz and Fergus, nodding as he pressed the call button for Leo, only the whites of his eyes and a black silhouette showing up in the moonlight, his hand twisted into a thumbs up as Leo answered.

'Argh, *ayunda, ayunda, rapido*, argh,' Chaz said in a

strained voice, while Fergus acted out the grunts and sounds of being attacked.

With Leo yelled 'Pepe' down the phone, Danny hung up and tossed it over his shoulder.

'Great performance,' Danny said, his teeth showing up as he grinned.

'Worthy of an Oscar nomination, I think,' said Chaz as all three of them turned their attention back to the villa below them.

Within a few seconds Leo appeared at the patio doors to the rear of the house. There was lots of shouting and arm waving, followed by the four armed men dotted around the garden running around the side of the villa towards the front gate.

'That's it. We've got probably three minutes before they find the two guys in the car and start heading back,' Danny said, leading the others to the back of the garden wall.

He turned to put his back against the wall and then bent his knees. Dropping the pump-action shotgun, Danny linked his fingers together and boosted Chaz up until he got his arm over the wall and pulled himself up. He did the same for Fergus, then picked up the shotgun up and handed it up to Chaz, who placed it on top of the wall. Reaching up, he grabbed Chaz and Fergus's wrists as they gripped his and pulled him up on top of the wall. The three of them dropped down into the darkness at the end of the garden, taking a second to scan their surroundings for movement. With no time for stealth, Danny exploded into a full sprint, followed by Chaz and Fergus, their shot-guns swinging from side to side in their hands as their legs pumped and feet pounded the soft manicured grass of Acosta's lawn. As they got close to the villa, Danny caught sight of Sandra, Louise and the back of Scott's head through the large glass bi-folding doors that spanned the back of the building.

Leaping over the steps that led up to the pool terrace, Danny's feet hit the ground just as Chavez turned on the kitchen stool. His eyes went wide at the sight of Danny and the others sprinting towards him. He went for his gun, grabbing the butt and pulling it from his shoulder holster. With his eyes locked on Chavez, Danny snapped his shotgun barrel ahead of him and pulled the trigger. Its heavy gauge shot punched a hole through the glass, blowing Chavez off his feet before bouncing him off the breakfast bar and onto the kitchen floor. Still running towards the villa, Danny put his arms up to cover his eyes and burst through the remaining fragmented glass still hanging in the door frame. He landed solidly in the kitchen while tiny crystallised glass beads bounced off the kitchen cupboards and worktops.

'Good evening, Daniel, nice of you to finally show up,' Scott said, pulling the memory stick out of the laptop before closing the lid down and sliding it back inside its bag.

'Sorry, Scotty boy, traffic was murder. Evening, ladies, shall we go?' Danny said as Chaz followed him in through the glassless frame, shotgun up and covering the door leading to the rest of the villa. Fergus stayed just outside, covering the back garden.

As Scott and the sisters stood up, the door to the kitchen burst open. One of Acosta's men, alerted by the sound of the shotgun, charged in from the hall. Stepping into his path, Chaz flipped the shotgun up and stabbed the butt hard into the guy's face. The blow whipped the man's head back with blood flicking in the air from his crunched-to-one-side nose. With his body's momentum continuing forward and his head flying backwards, the man's feet left the ground and he landed heavily on his back, out cold. Looking up from the unconscious man to see along the direction he'd entered from, Chaz saw Alonzo Acosta standing by the front door pointing a Croatian Agram 2000 submachine gun in his direction. Chaz dived behind the breakfast bar as Acosta opened fire on fully automatic, emptying the thirty-two round magazine in a fraction of a second. The deafening hail of bullets zinged down the hall and through the open door, missing Chaz by millimetres, apart from one round that blew a tuft of material from his overalls as it ripped through his flapping sleeve. They continued on their way across the kitchen before obliterating the glass in another bi-folding door. When the magazine clicked empty, Chaz pumped the shotgun and rolled across the floor, looking down the sights to see Acosta clicking a fresh magazine into the submachine gun. As Acosta lifted his head to take aim, Chaz took the shot. With the odd angle and quick reaction time, Chaz's aim was slightly off to hit him in the shoulder. Acosta thumped into the wall behind him, dropping the submachine gun as his arm hung by his side, useless. As Chaz pumped another cartridge into the chamber, Acosta spun off the wall and ran out of the front door, leaving a dragging smear of blood on the wall behind him.

'Change of plan. We're going out the front. Ferg, take point,' Danny yelled.

'Roger that,' Fergus said, running and jumping over Chaz to take up position on one side of the front door.

Chaz got to his feet and followed Fergus, taking up position on the other side of the open door while Danny ushered Scott and the two sisters into the hall after them.

Fergus and Chaz flicked their heads around the door then ducked back under cover, each taking a mental snapshot of Acosta running out the open gate, shouting at two of his men guarding the entrance as they waited for Leo and the others to return from investigating the call from Pepe.

'How are we looking?' Danny said over the top of the others.

'Two by the gate, one going through. I couldn't see anyone else,' Fergus shouted back.

'Vehicles?'

'Yeah, several on the drive.'

'Ok, keep their heads down while I see if I can find keys,' Danny said, heading for the table in the hall's corner.

'Roger that,' Fergus said, nodding to Chaz.

The unsaid understanding made them swing around both sides of the front door. With their shotguns up in front of them, they squeezed off a round, each blowing the render off the wall above Acosta's men on either side of the gate. Shocked, they ducked and ran out of the gate to take cover on the other side. Chaz and Fergus repeatedly pumped the shotguns, peppering the masonry and the open metal gate with shots.

'I'm out,' said Chaz.

'Me too,' Fergus said, chucking the shotgun on the floor and pulling both handguns out.

'Here,' Danny said, throwing his shotgun over to Chaz, who caught it and pumped another cartridge into the chamber.

'Got them,' Danny shouted, scooping up a set of keys from the drawer in the table.

His voice was drowned out by gunfire and bullets

ripping through the open doorway to tear strips of wood out of the staircase opposite.

'Persistent fuckers, aren't they?' Fergus grumbled to Chaz.

'Yeah, and I thought Spain was all about *mañana, mañana.*'

'You ready, guys? On three, yeah?' Danny shouted.

'Roger that,' Chaz and Fergus answered in unison.

'When we go, you stick to me like glue, ok?' Danny said to Scott and the two sisters.

'Roger that,' Scott said, trying to sound like Fergus and Chaz.

The sisters just huddled together and nodded.

'One, two, three.'

Chaz and Fergus moved around the door on three, Chaz pumping shots at Acosta's man poking around the right side of the gate, while Fergus charged out, both handguns up and firing at Acosta's man on the left, hitting him with two in the chest and one in the forehead. Danny came out behind them, pressing the button on the car keys until a Mercedes' indicators flash and it unlocked. They headed to the car, Danny climbing into the driver's seat while Scott and the two sisters jumped into the back. Chaz and Fergus, still covering the gate, headed for the car last, Fergus jumping in the front passenger seat, while Chaz dived on top of everyone in the back.

'Go, go, go!' Fergus shouted, lowering the window so he could cover them on the way out.

Danny hit the gas, spinning the wheels to spray gravel across the drive until the tyres found grip and the car shot out through the gate. Turning the steering wheel sharply, the tyres squealed on to the tarmac outside until they found grip and the car gained speed, running straight into

Acosta's men heading back from Pepe's car. Danny didn't flinch. Keeping his foot to the floor, he hit the men head on, sending two bouncing off the sides before flipping another up over the bonnet, smashing the windscreen before he bounced up over the roof to flop onto the road behind them. As Danny picked up speed, Fergus slid his torso up through the open window, firing his guns at Leo and Acosta making them duck down behind Pepe's car as they sped past, disappearing into the night.

CHAPTER 33

Twenty minutes later, Danny and the others parked up on a piece of wasteland just outside of Benidorm. Danny, Chaz and Fergus stripped out of their overalls, using the windscreen washer water to wet them and wash as much of the boot polish off their faces as possible. Once done, they bundled them and the caps into a pile and set light to them. While the blaze grew, they striped the weapons into pieces and threw the bits all around the wasteland. Chaz carried the cartridges and bullets and parts of the firing mechanisms over to the road and dropped them down the nearest drain so nobody could pick them up or re-assemble the weapons. Lastly, they pulled the latex gloves off and dropped them into the dying fire.

'Right, Scott, the memory stick,' Danny said with his hand out.

'Oh, yes, of course. I guess we hand this over to the authorities,' Scott said, giving it to Danny.

'Not exactly, mate,' Danny said, taking it and putting it into his pocket.

'What do you mean, not exactly?' Scott said.

'I had to do a deal with Delany. It was the only way we could find you and get you out,' Danny said, putting his hands up to calm Louise down when she immediately thought Danny was going to give her to Delany. 'Don't worry, it's just the memory stick. Delany has agreed to leave us alone, all of us. As long as he gets this memory stick back.'

'About the memory stick, I—'

'I don't want to hear it, Scott. I'm going to drop you at the airport so you can buy the tickets home. I'll do the exchange with Delany, then meet you back at the airport. No arguments,' Danny said, his face set like granite.

'But I've—' Scott tried to say.

'Scott, I said no argument. Now get in the car. The sooner we get out of here, the better.'

Scott reluctantly gave up and got into the car with the others. Everyone sat in silence on the way to Alicante airport, lost in reflective thoughts of the last few days. Before long, Danny pulled up outside departures and let them all out.

'Are you sure you don't want us to come with you?' Fergus said with Chaz standing beside him.

'No, you look after this lot. I won't be long. I'll do the exchange somewhere public, then get the hell out of there,' Danny said, managing a smile to his two closest friends.

'Ok, brother, be safe,' Chaz said, stepping back from the car.

They stood for a moment or two, watching Danny drive off into the distance, then turned and walking into the terminal to head for the nearest ticket desk.

As he headed back toward Benidorm, Danny called

Delany. He told him he had the memory stick and would meet him at the motorway services about ten miles outside of Benidorm.

CHAPTER 34

Driving at the speed limit, Danny cruised past the service station on the opposite side of the motorway, his face glued to the side window as he took in all the cars and people using the petrol pumps and parked up to use the services. Danny spotted where he wanted to do the handoff. It was public and covered by multiple CCTV cameras. Close to the spot, Danny saw Delany's car standing out like a sore thumb, a black Mercedes, the engine still running with the lights on and four people sitting patiently inside.

He drove on for five miles, sliding off at the next junction to circle around and head back towards the service station. A few minutes later, he took the services' slip road and drove past the petrol pumps to park up in front of the services building, directly in line with the CCTV camera for the entrance. He lowered the window and looked over to the shadowy occupants of the Mercedes parked thirty feet to his left. After a tense pause, the doors closest to him opened. The giant frame of Arlo got out of the back. He closed the door and just stood there with one hand on the butt of his gun under his coat. Delany got out of the front and stood for a while, just staring at Danny without moving. Getting out of the car, Danny walked halfway towards Delany, then stopped. Delany matched his steps until they stood facing each other.

'You have something for me?' Delany said with the stare of a man used to getting his own way.

'I'm a man of my word,' Danny said, matching his stare, the intensity of it eventually unnerving Delany, so he had to look away.

At that point, Danny reached into his pocket, moving slowly to keep Arlo from pulling his gun. He pulled out the memory stick between two fingers, holding it up until he saw Arlo relax the grip on his gun.

'Are we good?'

'I'm also a man of my word. We are good,' Delany said, taking the memory stick from Danny's fingers. 'You know, you're a handy guy. You made this lot look like a bunch of amateurs. I could use a man like you.'

'No, you couldn't,' Danny said, his face hard like granite and his eyes darkening angrily as he started walking backwards towards the car.

Delany stood where he was, a smile spreading across his face. 'Call me if you ever change your mind,' he called after Danny.

'I won't,' Danny growled, climbing back into the car.

Delany watched him reverse out of the parking space and drive off before turning and walking back to the car, spinning the memory stick over in his fingers. Danny headed back onto the motorway, checking behind him every few minutes in case Delany had him followed. He drove carefully and kept to the speed limit. The last thing he needed was to get pulled over for a broken windscreen in a stolen car from a gangland shootout. Thankfully, he reached the airport without incident. Pulling into the short stay car park, Danny locked the car and tossed the keys into a bin on the way to the airport's departure terminal.

'Oi, oi, here comes the stag,' came Fergus's unmistakable voice from Burger King.

'Everything taken care of?' Chaz asked as Danny joined them.

'Yeah, we're all good. You don't have to worry about Gregory Delany anymore,' Danny said, turning to Louise and Sandra, surprised by their subdued thanks, which he put down to not sinking in that they were free of Delany.

'Good job, old man. Here's your ticket. We've got a few hours to kill before the flight. Look, there's a traditional Spanish restaurant over there. Perhaps we could get something good to eat while we wait,' Scott said, turning his nose up at the Whopper burger Fergus was devouring next to him.

'Fuck that, you posh prick. There's a sports bar on the other side of security,' said Fergus, wiping burger juice from his chin with the back of his hand.

'Sounds good to me. All in favour of drinks in the sports bar?' said Chaz, winking at Sandra and Louise while he and Fergus shot their hands in the air.

Subdued, Louise and Sandra nodded their agreement.

'Motion carried. To the sports bar,' Chaz said, heading towards the security check to enter the departure lounge.

'Come on, Scotty boy, let me buy you a beer,' Danny said, putting his arm around his sulking mate to follow the others.

'How did it really go with that thug Delany?' Scott asked before they got to the sports bar.

TILL DEATH DO US PART

'Fine, it went fine. He got what he wanted and won't be bothering us again.'

'Mmm, good. He'll get his comeuppance soon enough,' Scott muttered under his breath.

'What? Just forget about it,Scott, let's have a few beers before we fly home and get back to normality. Oh, and I don't think we really need to tell Nikki all the gory details, do we?'

'My dear fellow, one shouldn't lie to one's sister, should one?' Scott said with a smug smile.

'If one's best friend is going to give one a black eye if he does, he should,' Danny said, giving Scott a threatening look before the two of them burst out laughing.

They joined the others in the sports bar where they stayed for several hours and several drinks, eventually piling out after the second call for their flight came over the speakers. After a short two-hour flight, they landed at Heathrow in the early hours of the morning. Tired and weary, they made their way through passport control and on into the arrivals hall.

'Scotty boy, are you staying at ours or going straight home?' Danny asked at the taxi rank.

'I think I'll go straight home, old man. I had quite enough excitement for one weekend. There's a good 50-year-old single malt whisky and my own bed waiting for me at home,' Scott said, climbing into a taxi.

'Ok mate, I'll talk to you later. Ladies, you take this one,' Danny said, opening the taxi door for them.

'Thank you,' Louise said.

'You're welcome,' Danny replied.

'No, I mean it, you're a good man. Nikki's a lucky woman,' Louise said.

'Go on, go home and try to forget about it,' Danny said.

'You can call me if you like,' Chaz said just before Danny shut the taxi door.

Sandra just smiled back and said, 'Bye Chaz.'

'She'll call, you think she'll call?' Chaz said to Fergus.

'Of course she'll call, mate,' Danny said, but somehow he didn't think she would. 'What about you two?' He continued as the sisters left and another taxi pulled up.

'We'll get the next one, you go. We'll see you during the week for the suit fitting,' Chaz said, letting Danny get the next cab.

'Ok will do, and mum's the word about Benidorm, or there might not be a wedding to wear any suits to.'

'What happens in Benidorm stays in Benidorm. Mum's the word, brother,' Chaz said.

Danny gave them a hug and slap on the back before getting in the taxi and heading across London towards home. He crept in around three in the morning, closing the door quietly before heading upstairs. Sliding out of his clothes, Danny eased into bed, breathing in the smell of clean sheets, then the smell of perfumed shampoo as he snuggled up behind Nikki.

'Oh, you're back,' she said sleepily, her hand reaching back to stroke his face as she moved back into his embrace.

Danny moved his head over and kissed her on the neck before resting his weary head on the pillow.

'Did you have a good time?' she said, barely awake.

'Yeah, it was a bit lively. Sorry to wake you, go back to sleep, love.'

'Mmm, ok,' she said dozing off.

CHAPTER 35

Leo walked into the IMED Levante hospital ward just after twelve noon the next day. He nodded to his man Pepe sitting guard outside the private room before he entered.

'How is the shoulder?' he said to Acosta, sitting up in the hospital bed, his shoulder all bandaged up after surgery to remove all the shot and repair the damage.

'They say it will heal in time. Did you take care of everything at the villa?' Acosta said, getting straight to the point.

'Yeah, we got rid of the bodies and cleaned up before the police arrived. I moved the money out of the safe and left it open. As far as they are concerned, it was a straight-forward armed robbery. I said they got away with thirty thousand euros. Four masked men, all white, average height, black clothing.'

'Good, good, they were here earlier but I was in surgery. They will be back later. Any news on Delany or the men from England?' Acosta said, wincing from the pain in his shoulder.

'No, Paulo says things have been really tight at the club since yesterday. Nobody's talking and nobody but Mendez's closest men have been allowed near the office. As for the English men and the women, there is no sign of them,' said Leo, looking out the window at a police car pulling into the car park below.

'Tell everyone to keep their eyes open. We don't know how much Delany knows or who the English men are working for.'

'Ok. The police are back,' Leo said, watching two officers walk from the car to the hospital entrance.

'You'd better go. Let me know if you find anything out.'

Leo nodded and headed out the door, stopping to look back at Acosta before leaving. 'Pepe is outside, just in case.'

'Thank you, Leo.'

'Keep your eyes open, Pepe, any trouble, you call me, ok?' Leo said once the door to the private room clicked shut.

'Yes, Mr Quinn.'

Leo left Pepe and walked along the long corridor towards the lifts and stairs. As he approached, the two officers he'd seen outside stepped out of the lift and walked up to the reception desk. Leo stepped into the empty lift and turned around to look at the officers as one of them asked a nurse where Acosta's room was. The other officer turned around and locked eyes with Leo as he waited for the lift doors to shut. They remained staring at each other until the lift doors closed, severing the tension. Something bothered Leo about the officers. He recognised him from somewhere but couldn't put his finger on where. By the time the lift doors opened on the ground floor, Leo had pushed it to the back of his mind. He'd seen a lot of police officers over the years, and a lot of police interview rooms, and the occasional inside of a cell. He could have seen the officer at any of these.

His phone buzzed with a message as he got into his car.

"Hey baby, you want to come over for some afternoon fun?"

He smiled at the thought of Marie and her lithe body. The pole dancer from the Nuevo Estilo gentleman's club was just what he needed after last night's disaster.

"On my way," he text back then headed out of the car park.

He smiled when the message read, "Let yourself in. I'll be waiting in the bedroom," came straight back.

Back up on the ward, Pepe spotted the two officers heading in his direction. He discreetly pulled the zip up on his jacket, conscious of the Glock 17 sitting in a shoulder holster underneath. He looked up at the officer in front like he was a lump of dog shit he'd just stepped in. The officer ignored his look and moved past him to the door to Acosta's room. Instead of going in, he stood by the door without opening it. Pepe suddenly got the feeling that something was off. As he moved to unzip his jacket, excruciating pain pulsed through his body from head to toe, every muscle painfully constricted, leaving him unable to move or make a sound other than a low groan. After seconds that felt like minutes, Pepe passed out. The second police officer standing behind him released the trigger on his teaser gun and put it away. The two of them quickly pushed Pepe upright in the chair, balancing him so it looked like he was sleeping. Satisfied, they left him and opened the door, entering Acosta's room.

'Good evening, Mr Acosta, we'd like to ask you some

questions about last night,' one officer said, the two of them splitting to move around to each side of the bed.

'You two can fuck off. I'm not saying anything without my lawyer present,' Acosta growled, a look of disdain on his face.

Acosta was about to say some more when the officer rammed a hand into his throat, pushing him flat on the bed, the realisation that both the police officers were wearing gloves re-enforcing the knowledge that he was in serious trouble. The next thing he knew was excruciating pain as the other officer gripped his wounded shoulder, digging his fingers in as hard as he could.

'Argh, fuck off, you're fucking dead, both of you,' Acosta spat, the hand around his throat choking his voice to a quiet rasp.

Releasing his shoulder, the officer grabbed Acosta's wrist, turning his back to him as he forced Acosta's arm out straight.

Still gripping Acosta's throat, the officer leaned in close to Acosta's ear and whispered, 'Mr Delany sends his regards.'

Acosta's eyes went wide, fear, panic and adrenaline masking the pain in his shoulder as he struggled to get free. He looked around the back of the officer holding his arm out straight. To his horror he saw and felt him push a hypodermic needle into his vein. As the officer pushed down the plunger, Acosta felt a euphoric wave ripple through his body before his eyes rolled back in his head, the large dose of pure heroin sending him under before he lost the ability to breathe and his heart stopped.

Leaving the needle hanging out of Acosta's arm, the two men went back into the corridor. They waited until a nurse moved away and disappeared into another room, then grabbed Pepe under each arm and took him into Acosta's room, shutting the door behind them. Pepe groaned as they pushed him on his front over the top of Acosta's body. The officer that had injected Acosta unzipped his stab vest and pulled out a silenced Beretta. He put it in Acosta's lifeless hand and curled his gloved fingers over the top of Acosta's hand. As he aimed it at Pepe's forehead, he opened his eyes. Before Pepe's brain could register what was happening, the officer pulled Acosta's finger back on the trigger and sent a bullet into Pepe's brain, the back of his head blowing out to leave a jet of bright red blood and bits of brain across the white sheets. Stepping back to survey their faked crime scene, the officers nodded to each other, satisfied it was good enough. One stepped over and hit the alarm button while the other one called in the murder of Alonzo Acosta by one of his own men over his radio.

CHAPTER 36

Leo drove through town still feeling unsettled. Over the last two days he'd lost three men, along with two more in hospital with the boss. The villa had been trashed and cars had been damaged and they had nothing to show for it. He had no idea who these British men worked for and no idea if Delany knew about their involvement in trying to hack his memory stick and gain control of his business. Leo had worked for Alonzo Acosta for many years and was a loyal man, but trouble like this starts the cogs of the brain turning. Maybe this was a good time to think about an exit strategy and retirement. Pushing those thoughts aside in favour of an afternoon of pleasure, Leo parked up outside the apartment complex. The residents were mainly locals, and the complex was set way back from the beach and tourist hotels, making it quiet at this time of day. Leo walked through the passageway into a large courtyard surrounded on all sides by apartments. Taking the stairs with a spring in his step, he headed along the walkway until he came to Marie's apartment. Following Marie's instructions, Leo pushed the door to find the latch clicked back, letting it swing open. He went inside and closed the door behind him, releasing the latch so the door locked shut.

'Hey, Marie, you ready for me, baby?' he said, heading for the bedroom.

'Marie!' he said again, pushing the bedroom door open.

Marie lay in her underwear, spread eagle on the bed, her hands and feet tied tightly to the four wooden legs, her eyes looking up at him, wide in panic as she let out a muffled screams through her taped-up mouth.

'Oh shit,' Leo muttered, forgetting all about Marie in favour of self-preservation.

He immediately went for his gun as he turned to head for the front door but instead of seeing the bright sunlight through its glass panelling, he saw the massive outline of Arlo and the wooden grain of a baseball bat a split second before it made contact with his head. The blow flattened him to the ground. The gun, barely out of his holster, dropped onto the tiled floor, where Arlo kicked it out of the way. Leo instinctively brought his knees and hands up to protect himself, the soft flesh offering little protection against Arlo's barrage of blows.

Pain turned into dull shock, then shock turned into a dull, semi-conscious state just before he passed out. Leo woke up shivering and in a world of pain with no idea how long he'd been out. Disorientated, and with blood rushing to his head, Leo opened the one eye that wasn't swollen shut. The first thing he saw was the upside down view of Marie lying motionless in her underwear in a pool of blood on the freezing concrete floor, her body beaten and broken, with a look of terror locked on her face from the moment Arlo cut her throat. With his hands bound behind his back, Leo swung around in pain as chains suspended from the ceiling dug into his ankle. He looked past Marie to see Mendez, Arlo and Delany lined up in the middle of their men in the back room of the Helado de Frutas ice cream factory. Mendez walked forward, moving around the pool of blood surrounding Marie until he was close to Leo. He squatted down on his haunches and looked Leo in the eye.

'I've put up with a lot of shit from you and Alonzo over the years, but this time you've crossed the line and there's no going back,' he said in a calm, low voice.

'What the fuck are you talking about? We've done nothing,' Leo spluttered out, holding on to the slim chance that this was an elaborate trick to make him talk.

Mendez reached forward and grabbed Leo's shoulders, swinging him around until he could see the body of Paulo Ramos hanging upside down beside him, his face beaten to a pulp and a bullet hole in his forehead.

'We know everything, Leo,' Mendez said, letting go of Leo so he swung back and forth as he walked back.

'Well fucking get on with it then,' Leo shouted in defiance.

Next, Delany walked forward and squatted down to look Leo in the face. Arlo followed him before stepping out of sight behind Leo.

'You speak English, yes?' he said gruffly, while slapping Leo on the cheek.

'Yes, I speak English,' Leo spat back.

'Good, I'm a very powerful man, Leo, and as a powerful man, I have a certain reputation to uphold. I can't let people take the piss without taking action, can I?'

'Fuck off, you English bastard,' Leo grunted, violently swinging his head forward to try and headbutt Delany.

Delany dodged back and cracked a punch to the bridge of Leo's nose, clouding his vision with stars and tears.

'Enjoy hell, you Spanish prick,' Delany said as Leo's vision returned.

Leo opened his mouth to shout more insults, but was cut short by a clear plastic bag sliding up over his head from behind. Arlo twisted the back of the bag so it pulled tightly over Leo's face, distorting his features. He tried to breathe, but the bag just sucked in over his mouth. Looking through the bag with his one good eye, all he could see was the blurry vision of Delany smiling back at him. With his lungs burning and panic setting in, Leo thrashed around, his body jerking while Arlo kept a tight grip on the bag. Eventually the movement slowed and the world went dark for Leo. Arlo held him in place until Leo's heart stopped and the last twitch of life left his body.

'That's the end of that. Clean this shit up,' Delany said to Mendez's men as he walked away.

Delany, Mendez and Arlo walked out of the factory and got into a waiting car which sped away as soon as they were in.

'Take us back to the club,' Mendez said to the driver.

'Good. Tonight we drink and put all this behind us. Tomorrow I'll fly back to the UK. Then it's business as usual,' said Delany in a more cheerful mood.

CHAPTER 37

anny woke up to the sound of music and the smell of bacon, both equally welcome as they assaulted his senses. He rolled over and picked up his trusty G-Shock watch, rubbing his eyes until the hands at ten past eleven came into focus. He rolled out of bed and stretched, arching his back and flexing his shoulders to a host of clicks, cracks and nagging pain from multiple old wounds.

That was the last time. No more. I'm too old for this shit.

Yawning, he pulled on some jogging bottoms and an old T-shirt, then headed downstairs, smiling to himself as he followed the sound of the future Mrs Pearson singing to the radio in the kitchen. Rolling his feet silently on the tiled hall floor, Danny peeped through the open kitchen door. Nikki had her back to him, busily singing to herself as she boiled the kettle to make tea. Danny moved towards her slowly, his hands out to grab her around the waist. He got within two feet of her before she spun around.

'Not even close. I heard your old bones creaking a mile off,' she grinned.

'Oi, I'm not that old, and I know I didn't make a sound,' Danny said, pretending to look hurt.

'Yeah, I know. Spatial awareness, you know, like you taught me. Allow your mind to pick up on anything out of place. I saw you coming in the reflection off the kettle,' she said, sliding her arms around his neck before giving him a kiss.

'Mmm, and there's me thinking you weren't listening,' Danny said, hugging her tight.

'You're losing your touch, old man, all it took was a packet of bacon and a mug of tea and you fell right into my trap,' she said, turning back to finish the tea and slide the bacon out of the oven.

'Yeah, you could be right,' Danny said with a melancholy look on his face.

'Are you alright?' she said, picking up on the tone of his voice.

'Er, what? Oh yeah, I'm fine, just tired. Thanks, love,' he said as she placed the mug of tea and bacon sandwich in front of him.

'Ah, yes, the infamous stag do. Come on then, how was it? Oh, and where's your suitcase?'

'The airport lost them. They're probably sunning themselves in the Maldives as we speak. There's nothing important in them, only a few old clothes. I'll call the airline later. As for the weekend, I'm sworn to secrecy. What happens on the stag do, stays on the stag do. All I'll say is it was lively,' Danny lied, taking a big bite out of his sandwich before Nikki pushed him further.

'Ok, ok, I can take a hint, but when I'm away next weekend for my hen do, don't expect me to be giving you a blow by blow account,' she said, grinning across the kitchen table at him.

'I wouldn't have it any other way,' Danny said, returning the grin.

After some sleep and now a belly full of food, Danny started to forget about the disastrous weekend and focus on the present.

'What do you want to do today?' he asked Nikki.

'You, Mr Pearson, will have to entertain yourself. I'm going for my last dress fitting with the girls. In fact, I'd better get going,' she said, giving him a peck on the cheek before heading out into the hall to get her things. She poked her head around the kitchen door a few minutes later, 'Call your brother and congratulate him on the new baby.'

'Baby, shit, I forgot about that. What did they have a boy or a girl?'

'Forgot! God, how drunk did you get out there? You have a new niece called Evie.' Nikki said walking back out into the hall.

'Yeah, sorry. Brain like a sieve. I'll call him in a bit,' Danny shouted after her.

'OK. Gotta go, bye,' she shouted back, shutting the front door behind her.

Danny drummed his fingers on the kitchen table, listening to the sound of the empty house.

'Right call Rob, then what? Em, Big Dave's Gym it is then,' he said, finishing his sandwich and tea before heading upstairs to get his gym kit ready.

CHAPTER 38

Delany entered Heathrow's terminal 5 the next day. After the short flight in British Airways business class seating, he text a message as he passed through security, his knuckles white from gripping onto the handle of his hand luggage tightly through passport control. He relaxed a little as he left the arrivals hall for the pickup zone. A silver Bentley Bentayga glided into view, stopping silently beside him. The driver hopped out and moved swiftly around to take the bag and open the door for him.

'Thank you, Tyson. I'll look after the bag,' Delany said, not wanting to let the memory stick out of his sight, even if it was only in the boot.

'Yes, Mr Delany,' Tyson replied, shutting the door for Delany before getting back in the driver's seat. 'Where to?'

'Home please, Tyson. Everything been ok while I was away?'

'Yes sir, Ken's had everything running like clockwork, no problems.'

'Good,' Delany replied, feeling in a good mood now he

was back on his own patch, in control of his empire, his kingdom.

Half an hour later, the driver turned through the opening gates to Delany's Georgian mansion in Twickenham. When he got out of the car, Tyson drove the Bentley into the large garage, the chair and bloodstains from Patrick Hopkins' beating all cleaned away to leave a shiny painted floor. Delany opened the front door, pausing to watch the electric gates close before entering and heading across the hallway into the kitchen. Kenneth Gambit paced up and down on the far side, his mobile phone glued to his ear as he spoke aggressively to whoever was on the other end.

'Problem, Ken?' Delany said, dumping his bag on the kitchen's marble worktop.

'Stay on the line, don't you go fucking anywhere,' Gambit growled down the phone before turning to face Delany. 'Birmingham came up light again. Someone's been dipping their fingers, boss.'

'Is that Dwaine? You tell him to find out who it is and deal with it.'

'Yes, boss.'

'And tell him to make up the shortfall out of his own pocket. I'm not paying for his problem.'

'Yes, boss,' said Gambit, returning to the call to shout Delany's orders at Dwaine.

When he'd finished, he hung up and pocketed his phone. He walked over to Delany who was making a cappuccino on the coffee machine built into the kitchen cabinets. Ken had a look that didn't match the expensive business suits he dressed in. His hands were large and covered in black prison ink tattoos, the words and patterns across the knuckles distorted, lost under crisscrossed, battle-earned scarring. Deeply furrowed lines etched their way across his face from his permanent frown. His eyes were always narrowed, the irises so dark they blended with his pupils as if they were one, cold and lifeless like a shark.

'Did you get everything sorted in Spain?'

'All sorted,' Delany said, unzipping his bag to pull out the memory stick and wave it in front of Ken.

'And Louise?'

'Don't worry about it. She won't be back. Forget her,' Delany said, his mannerisms and voice telling Ken that he should leave that subject alone.

'Of course, boss, good to have you back.'

'Where's Hopkins?'

'At home, do you want me to fetch him in?'

Delany looked at the time on his watch and thought about it before answering.

'No, get him in tomorrow. I'll just lock this in the safe, then you can run me over to the new development. I want to see how it's coming along.'

'I'll get the Range Rover out of the garage. You might want to change boss, the site's still pretty muddy after last week's rain.'

'OK, thanks ken.'

After Ken left the room, Delany took his cappuccino and the memory card into his office. He put the coffee on his desk and walked over to the wood panelling on the far side of the room. Pressing the middle panel firmly until it popped out on one side, he pulled it open and reached in putting his thumb on a fingerprint reader set in a steel door. After a whir from the motors retracting the safe's locking bars, the door popped forward an inch. Delany pulled it all the way open and placed the 256-bit AES encryption, military-grade USB memory stick next to its twin, on top of a stack of bundled fifty pound notes and sensitive files and a selection of burner phones. He locked the safe and clicked the panel back into place, then picked up his coffee. Finishing it on his way through the kitchen, he put the cup in the dishwasher and went and got changed before heading out to Ken who was waiting in the ticking-over Range Rover on the drive.

CHAPTER 39

'Scott's here,' Nikki shouted down from the bedroom.

'Ok, got it,' Danny shouted back as he headed from the kitchen to get the front door, opening it just as Scott reached out to knock.

'Morning, Daniel, you look well rested after all the shenanigans of last weekend,' Scott said, walking inside the house.

'Exactly what shenanigans are we talking about?' Nikki said, hearing Scott as she came down the stairs.

'Ah, hello sis. You know, dodging bad guys, car chases and gunfights, the usual type of thing,' Scott said with a chuckle, while Danny gave him a look like daggers.

'Don't tell me then,' Nikki joked, ignoring the comment as she headed into the kitchen. 'You want a tea or coffee, Scott?'

'We haven't got time, love, we've got to go. Chaz and Fergus are meeting us at the suit shop,' Danny said, pushing Scott back towards the door.

STEPHEN TAYLOR

'Ok, you'll be back before I go to Tara's, won't you?' she called back.

'Yeah, I'll be back in plenty of time. See you later,' Danny said, following a smirking Scott towards his car.

'Hey, aren't you forgetting something?' Nikki called after him.

'Er, what?' Danny turned back to Nikki as she came to the front door.

'We're not even married yet and already I'm not getting kisses goodbye.'

'Sorry, love. Trying to organise your brother and the lads is worse than looking after kids,' he said, giving her a kiss goodbye.

'Good lord, you two, put her down and come on,' Scott shouted from his new Porsche Cayenne Turbo.

'See you later,' Danny said with a grin as he pulled away from Nikki and walked around Scott's car to get in the passenger seat.

'What are you playing at, Scott? You nearly gave me a heart attack with all that bad guy and gunfights bollocks,' Danny said as they pulled away.

'Sorry, old man, just having a little fun. No harm done.'

'Alright, I suppose not. Just give it a rest with the wind-ups, mate. I'm trying to forget last weekend ever happened.'

'Mmm, any time now, Gregory Delany's going to wish it never happened as well,' Scott muttered under his breath.

'What was that, Scotty?' Danny said, catching Delany's name.

'Nothing, dear boy, let's just say sometimes there's a more subtle way to sort things out than brute force and bullets.'

160

Danny was going to ask him what he meant by that, but it was a nice day and he was in too good a mood to be trying to work out Scott's intellectual cryptic gibberish. Plus, they were going to get the suits for his wedding, so he decided against it.

Chaz and Fergus were already there when they got to the suit shop.

'Morning guys,' Danny said as he entered the shop.

'What do you reckon, Ferg?' said Chaz.

'Aye, he's still smiling. I reckon the missus still doesn't know about last weekend and the wedding's on,' Fergus said with a chuckle.

'Very funny, and no she doesn't know, so let's keep it that way, ok?'

'Fine with me,' Fergus said.

'Mum's the word, mate. My lips are sealed,' Chaz added.

'Where's the shopkeeper?' Danny asked.

'He's out back fetching the suits. That's three large and one to fit a small child,' Fergus said, grinning at Scott.

'Oh very droll. I hope he's let the arms out so you can scrape your knuckles on the floor without shirt cuffs showing,' Scott snapped back, unable to stifle a smile when Fergus started laughing at his comment.

'You know what? I think he's starting to grow on me,' Fergus said to Chaz.

CHAPTER 40

By the time Patrick Hopkins arrived at the mansion, Gregory Delany had been up for hours. He'd been on the burner phones from the safe, checking on his distribution network. The calls weren't necessary, but Delany wanted to reinforce the message that he was back and it was business as usual. Ken opened the door for Hopkins, standing just far enough out of his way so Hopkins could only get past by turning sideways to get in. Ken followed Hopkins with a smirk on his face, the slowly-healing, puffy, purple bruises on Hopkins's face from the beating still amusing him. He watched Hopkins go into the office, then went into the lounge to find Delany.

'Hopkins is here.'

'Good. How does he look?' Delany asked.

'Like shit, he'll be alright in a few more days.'

Delany didn't answer. He just nodded his head and headed for the office, opening the door slowly to let his gaze fall on Hopkins with maximum intimidating effect.

'Last week was last week, Patrick. You took your

punishment and I don't hold a grudge. So let's move on, business as usual.'

'Yes, Mr Delany,' Hopkins replied, avoiding Delany's gaze, as he didn't have the nerve to maintain eye contact.

'Good.' Delany walked across the room and popped the wooden panel forward before opening the safe and retrieving the two memory sticks. He handed the one he got back from Danny to Hopkins and put the other on the office desk. 'Check that it's undamaged, then update them both with the new figures.'

'Yes, Mr Delany,' Hopkins said, turning his laptop on before slotting the memory stick into the port at the side.

Almost out of the door, Delany stopped and turned back when the laptop started making a loud beeping sound.

'What's going on?'

'I don't know, the screen's gone blank.'

Delany moved up beside Hopkins, as he tapped the escape key with no effect. As they stood trying to figure it out, streams of code and commands scrolled across the laptop in green words, symbols and numbers.

'What's the matter with this thing, is the laptop on the blink?' Delany grumbled, tapping the side of the screen impatiently.

He stopped abruptly when the words 'Copy complete' came up on the latest command line, quickly superseded by the word 'Uploading'. A progress bar appeared above a cascading stream of email addresses, hitting forty percent done before they figured out what was going on. Delany's eyes went wide when he saw where the information was being directed, Scotland Yard, drug enforcement agencies, MI5, MI6, a whole host of .gov email addresses and all the paper and media agencies, a tick showing at the end of each address just before the next one appeared.

'Pull the memory stick. Shit, pull the fucking stick,' flapped Delany.

He grabbed the memory stick, yanked it out of the laptop and stared at the screen.

The upload bar continued to scroll across.

'Shit, turn the laptop off quickly.'

Hopkins tried, but the keys on the keyboard had no effect. The virus Scott had programmed into the memory stick at Acosta's villa was doing its job perfectly.

'Fuck, disconnect the internet. Turn it off. Do something,' Delany yelled, finally picking up the laptop in a fit of frustration and rage and smashing it on the corner of the desk.

Keys flew off the keyboard, and the screen cracked before he dumped it back down on the desk. As he looked at the partly visible screen, only the *a* and *d* of '*Upload*' and all of the word '*complete*' were clearly visible.

Delany dropped the laptop and stood upright. The colour drained from his face as the enormity of what had just happened sunk in. Thirty seconds later he exploded into action like he'd been struck by lightning.

'Ken, Ken, get your arse in here,' he yelled throwing the panel in the wall open and hurriedly opening the safe.

'Boss,' said Ken as he rushed in.

'You and Tyson bring the cars around. We've got to get out of here, now. Oh, and bring Billy as well,' Delany shouted, grabbing a sports holdall from the corner of the room. He shook all the gym kit out and started filling it with the files, cash and a Glock 17 from the safe. Ken left, puzzled, but knew better than to question his boss so just did as he was told. Slamming the safe shut, Delany grabbed the second memory stick and threw it at Hopkins, who caught it with shaking hands.

'You. Get my laptop over there. You're coming with us,' Delany gestured to the other desk in the room. 'There's a mobile Wi-Fi dongle in the bag. Start moving money, anywhere that can't be touched or frozen. Now,' he shouted, shaking Hopkins into action before running upstairs to throw some clothes into the sports bag.

A couple of minutes later, they exited the front door, Delany pushing Hopkins in front of him to the waiting car.

'Follow us,' he shouted to Tyson and Billy in the second car.

'Where to, boss?' said Ken, looking back from the driver's seat.

'Mersea Island, Essex, I bought a holiday home for that bitch, Louise. It's under a shell company name. No one knows I've got it.'

'Do you mind me asking what's going on, boss?' Ken asked from the driver's seat.

'That fucking guy Pearson, he screwed us all over. Send the copy of his passport photo to everyone. I'll give a hundred grand to the first person who kills that son of a bitch. I want him dead like yesterday, and I want proof that it's done.'

After sending Danny's passport picture to Ken's phone, Delany scrolled through his contacts as he tried to figure out his next course of action. He looked across at Hopkins, who was sitting as far away from him as he could in the back of the car, trying to look invisible.

'Who told you to stop fucking working? Get my money somewhere safe. Any second now, the authorities will get a court order and freeze my assets, so fucking move your arse and transfer my money somewhere safe.'

With shaky hands Hopkins went back to tapping the keyboard of the laptop, all the time wishing he'd never gotten involved with Gregory Delany.

While flying through the suburbs of London, Delany's phone rang with DCI Cain's number appearing on the caller ID.

'Yes,' Delany grunted.

'I don't know what the fuck's going on, but you've got the National Crime Agency and an armed response unit on the way to your house right fucking now. You've got about five minutes to get the fuck out of there and disappear. This is it, we're finished, don't ever contact me again.'

'Now you listen to me, you little shit. We're finished when I say we're finished. I've got plenty on you and if I go down, you're coming with me,' Delany yelled back down the phone.

There was silence on the line, but Delany knew Cain hadn't hung up on him. He took a few deep breaths before continuing.

'I'm already away from the house. As soon as I'm safe, I'll make arrangements to get out of the country until I can sort this mess out. Somewhere with no extradition treaty. I have friends in the Sudan. In the meantime, you keep your ear to the ground. If they're getting close to me, I want to know. Do you hear me, Cain?' Delany said, his voice a little calmer.

'Yes, Mr Delany,' Cain replied after another tense silence.

'And Cain, I've put a hit out on Pearson. If you find him and kill him before anyone else does, I'll destroy everything I have on you. You'll be a free man.' Delany said hanging up before Cain could answer.

CHAPTER 41

'No, lads, I've got to go. I've got to catch Nikki before she leaves for her hen weekend,' Danny said, this being his third attempt to get out of the pub before Scott, Fergus, and Chaz brought another round of drinks.

'Do you want me to drive you?' said Scott.

'Christ no, you've had way too much to drink. Seriously, get a cab home, Scott. I'm going to walk. I need the fresh air,' Danny said, getting up onto his feet before they could talk him out of going.

'That's it, you run along. I don't need you anyway. I've got my new best mate Scott here. Isn't that right, Scott, me old mate?' Fergus said loudly, slapping Scott on the back while winking and grinning at Danny.

'Absolutely, old chap. Another drink, anyone?' said Scott, to cheers from Fergus and Chaz.

'Just make sure he gets a cab home, ok? I'll see you guys just before the wedding,' Danny said, pointing at Scott before rolling his eyes when they all cheered again.

Leaving the pub, Danny headed along the High Street

towards home. Three youths on Sur-Ron E-bikes came whizzing down the high street, all three obviously gang members in their matching black sport jackets, baggy jeans and shiny white new trainers. They wore motocross helmets over balaclavas, so only their eyes were visible. Dreadlocks flapping in the wind from under the crash helmet singled the lead rider out from the others. Danny watched them in his peripheral vision, more out of curiosity than apprehension. He'd seen them riding around before, heard the stories of phones and bikes being stolen and drugs being dealt on the estates. Just before they rode past on the other side of the road, Danny caught Dreadlocks' head turn his way and his eyes lock onto him. The hairs on the back of Danny's neck stood up when Dreadlocks' head didn't turn away from him. He still had the feeling that eyes were on him as the youths continued down the high street and out of his field of vision.

Without turning, Danny ducked into a newsagents. He picked up a paper and paid for it, looking back down the road at the youths through the shop window as he waited for his change. They'd pulled over in a bus stop bay twenty metres down the road, their heads all turned back to look in his direction. Dreadlocks slid his helmet up, so it sat on the very top of his balaclava while he talked on a mobile phone. As Danny watched, a bus came down the high street and started pulling into the bus stop. The driver edged forward, making hand signals for the youths to move out of the bus bay. They stuck their fingers up and shouted at the driver before begrudgingly moving forward out of the bus's way. The bus driver pulled forward, briefly blocking the line of sight from the youths and Danny in the newsagents. Danny didn't waste a second. He spun out of the newsagents' door and turned off the high street down Truro road. Pulling out his phone and tapped a number as he broke into a flat-out sprint.

'Mate, you've seen the news then,' said a slightly drunk Chaz, his voice raised over the noise in the pub.

'What? No, what news?' Danny answered through gulps of air.

'It's on the TV now, pictures of Gregory Delany, the cocaine king. Scott stitched him right up. His whole drug organisation, everything on the memory stick emailed to every newspaper, police department, government official. He's public enemy number one. There's a massive manhunt out for him.'

'Where's Scott?' Danny gasped.

'He's taken a cab home. What's up?' Chaz said, Danny's breathing and the tone of his voice setting off alarm bells.

'Something's wrong. I've just been eyeballed by a street gang on the high street.'

'What? Where are you? We're on our way,' Chaz said, immediately sobering up, with Fergus doing the same as he caught snippets of the conversation.

'No, it's fine. I think I lost them. Look, I'm going back home to check on Nikki. Tell Fergus to do the same. Take his wife and kids to her mother's, make sure they are safe. You go after Scott and call Sandra and Louise to make sure they are ok. We can meet up later and figure out if we have anything to worry about.'

'We're leaving now. Stay safe, brother,' Chaz said, hanging up and cocking his head to Fergus to follow him out of the pub.

CHAPTER 42

Danny glanced behind him, relieved to see the road was clear all the way back to the high street in the distance. He slowed to a walk on Truro Road to catch his breath as he approached Eldon Road running across a little way in front of him. He turned right at the junction and walked along Eldon Road knowing Erskine Road was just ahead of him, and his house only a few minutes away. As Danny approached Erskine Road, Dreadlocks and the two other bikers rounded the corner and fanned out blocking the road, with Dreadlocks in the middle. The bikes on either side of Dreadlocks now had a pillion passenger behind the rider, all dressed in their urban gang uniform. Their eyes glinted through the balaclavas, high on pack mentality and frenzied excitement.

Danny stood his ground. There was no point running. He couldn't outrun the fast electric Sur-Ron bikes. He calmed his breathing and allowed his mind to tick over various attack and defensive strategies. As he watched like a hawk, the pillion passengers pulled large, elaborately shaped zombie knives from their jackets. Dreadlocks swung his head from side to side, nodding to the rider to go. With an electric whine, the two bikes took off, accelerating surprisingly fast. One rider bumped up the kerb and sped along the footpath towards Danny. His pillion passenger standing up on the rear foot pegs, the zombie knife raised in one hand while he gripped the back of the rider's jacket to steady himself. The other bike sped along the road, the rider and pillion's heads visible above the parked cars as it approached.

When the bike on the path got to within a few feet, Danny jumped in between two parked cars on his left. The pillion leaned over and swiped the razor-sharp blade as he passed, the blade glinting millimetres from Danny's cheek. With the bike on the roadside bearing down on him and no time to think, Danny slammed himself backwards onto the bonnet of the parked car behind him, the lights flashing and alarm going off as the blade swung by the pillion swished over the top of him. Danny popped himself upright like a figure out of a jack-in-a-box. Somewhere behind him, he could hear the tyres of the e-bikes locking up and sliding as his attackers spun around for another approach.

Looking down, Danny saw a cast iron drain by the kerb. He ducked down and slid his fingers through the slots, curling them around underneath as he pulled with all his might. The cast iron drain cover was heavy, weighing around twenty kilos as it popped out of its slot. With one eye on the fast approaching bike on the pavement, Danny heaved the cover clear of the parked cars, swinging it around with both hands before releasing it into the air space just in front of the bike.

The combination of the flying cover and speed of the

bike made the contact all the more devastating. The corner of the cover struck the rider square in the chest, breaking three ribs as it stopped him in mid air. His bike shot out from underneath him, smashing into a parked van while the rider and the pillion passenger crunched onto their backs on the pavement. Danny sprung out from between the cars and stamped on the pillion passenger's wrist as he lay winded and stuck under the semi-conscious rider. He let go of the zombie knife, which Danny kicked away before reaching under the youths helmet and tearing it off his head. Before he could say anything, Danny smashed the helmet repeatedly into the youth's balaclava covered face. His nose collapsed and his eyes rolled back in his head.

The bike that was roadside slowed. Its rider and pillion passenger stood up on the foot pegs, trying to see over the top of the parked cars at where their gang mates had gone. Their eyes went wide when Danny, fuelled on adrenaline and pure rage, exploded into view, leaping onto the car bonnet with a crash helmet grasped in one hand and the zombie knife in the other. The rider twisted the throttle, but was too late. Danny launched himself off the bonnet, the crash helmet in his hand crunching into the pillion's crash helmet, knocking his head ninety degrees sideways. Danny's other arm hooked around the front of the rider to thump the blade of the zombie knife through his jacket, embedding it into his shoulder. The bike and all three of them went over onto the tarmac. Danny was first up, kicking the pillion passenger in the balls to keep him down. Darting forward, Danny grabbed the knife in the rider's shoulder and twisted it as he pulled it out, leaving the rider screaming and rolling around on the floor in agony.

Bending down to pick up the pillion's dropped knife, Danny stood upright and faced Dreadlocks sitting on his bike at the end of the road. With his face set and eyes narrowed he stared into Dreadlocks' eyes, Danny raised the zombie knives and started walking straight towards the youth. Surprise and fear crept into Dreadlocks' eyes. He locked the handlebars and spun the bike around before speeding off, leaning the bike over around the corner until he disappeared out of sight. Danny turned. The rider of the bike had taken off his helmet and balaclava with his good arm before kicking the bike off his leg. Danny grabbed him as he got on to his knees, trying to stand, his arm hanging limp by his side from the stab wound in his shoulder. He froze, snivelling and crying, when Danny touched the cold steel of the zombie knife to the side of his neck.

'You work for Gregory Delany?' Danny said in a low growl.

'Don't hurt me, man, we work for Lionel. It's Lionel that works for Delany.'

'Lionel's the dreadlock guy on the bike?' Danny said, moving the knife along the skin just enough to nick it.

'Don't, man, please. Yeah, Lionel was on the other bike,' stuttered the youth, shaking.

'Who else have you been looking for? Three men? Two women?'

'Nah, I don't know anything about anyone else. Just you. Lionel was offering 10k for the first one to kill you. He sent us this, look.' The youth pulled his phone out of his baggy jeans and showed Danny a copy of his photocopied passport from Benidorm.

'Where can I find Lionel?' Danny ordered.

'He runs the Hazlewood estate. You'll find him there.'

'Runs? He's a dealer?'

'Yeah, for Mr Delany.'

Danny took the knife away from the youth's neck and walked over to the open drain cover between the parked cars. He dropped the knives into the black stinking water in the drain, looked at the youths rolling about on the pavement and then across at the ones in the road.

'Call yourselves an ambulance,' Danny said, walking off. A few feet on he shouted over his shoulder, 'If I see you again, I'll kill you.'

CHAPTER 43

Danny approached his house with caution. There had been no signs of anyone for the rest of the walk home and his road was quiet, with no unfamiliar vehicles parked along it. He moved up to his front door, keeping to one side so his outline didn't show through the mottled glass in the centre of the door. Easing the key into the lock, he gently clicked the Yale lock until the door popped open a crack. Danny put his ear to the gap and listened to the sounds of the house, breathing a sigh of relief when he heard the kitchen radio playing and Nikki singing badly to one of her favourite tunes.

'Hi, I'm home,' he shouted, walking in like nothing had happened.

'About time. I thought I was going to have to leave without seeing you,' Nikki said, coming into the hall, her face looking at him oddly when she saw him looking dishevelled, hot and sweaty. 'Anything you want to tell me?' she added.

'What, oh, no. You know what Ferg and Chaz are like. They dragged me into a pub after the suit fitting and I lost track of time. I had to run all the way home, so I didn't miss you,' Danny said, wiping the sweat off his forehead.

'Well, you only just made it. Tara will be here any minute to pick me up,' Nikki said, standing on tiptoes to give Danny a kiss on the lips before running upstairs to get her bags.

'Great, eh, I mean, I'm glad I made it,' Danny shouted up the stairs to her while stepping into the lounge to check for anything out of place out of the window, only to see Tara pull up in her Mini. 'Tara's here.'

'Ok,' replied Nikki, struggling with her bags down the stairs.

'Here, let me help you,' Danny said, running up to grab her bags.

He helped her out to the car and put the bags in the back.

'This is it. Next time I see you, it'll be our wedding day,' Nikki said with a grin.

'Enjoy your hen do, love, I'll see you at the church,' Danny said, giving her a hug, his eyes scanning up and down the road over her shoulder.

When they separated, they kissed, and Nikki got into her friend's car. Danny waved them off, his face falling the moment she rounded the corner and disappeared out of sight. Grabbing his phone, he hurried back inside.

'Chaz, is everyone safe?'

'Yes, mate, all quiet here. I've sent Gaynor and the kids to her mother's. Fergus just called. He's at Scott's, all quiet there as well.'

'Good, I ran into some trouble on the way home.'

'You ok?' Chaz said, concerned.

'Yeah, I'm fine. The bad news is Delany put a price on

my head. The good news is it looks like it's only me he's after.'

'We're in this together, brother, you, me and Ferg. What do you want us to do?'

'You and Ferg still got some tools stashed away?' Danny said, his eyes looking up the stairs as he thought of his go bag with money, passports and a Glock 17 handgun hidden under the panel in the bottom of his wardrobe.

'Yeah, of course.'

'Good, get them. Scott's got a second apartment he sometimes rents out to corporate customers. Meet me there in a couple of hours.'

'Roger that. What are you going to do?'

'There's a local dealer who works for Delany. I'm going to see if he knows where his boss is. Then I'm going to find him and kill him. No Delany, no price on my head,' Danny said without emotion.

'Roger that. I'll see you in a little while,' Chaz said, totally unfazed by Danny's plans.

Danny hung up and moved to the stairs, heading to get his go bag. As he put one foot on the bottom step, there was a knock on the front door. He stepped back down, sliding his hand into the umbrella stand in the hall. His fingers curled around an old baseball bat he always kept in there for emergencies.

The knock came again, the jagged outline of two men visible through the mottled glass panel in the front door. 'Can you open the door, please, Mr Pearson. It's the police,' came a muffled voice.

Danny moved to the door, planting his foot down a little way behind it so nobody could barge inside when he opened the latch. With the baseball bat held just out of sight behind the door, Danny opened it a crack and peered out through the gap.

'DCI Cain and Detective Wade,' said the man on the other side while flashing his ID badge through the crack in the door.

'What do you want?' Danny said, unimpressed.

'We have information to suggest that your life might be in danger, Mr Pearson, and we'd like to take you to the station for your own safety, and to help us with our enquiries,' Cain said, his tone and face telling Danny it wasn't a request, it was a demand.

Danny didn't move for a few seconds, his face tense and eyes looking straight into Cain's. 'Ok,' he finally said, carefully placing the baseball bat up against the hall wall behind the door before opening it wide and stepping outside. Cain opened the back door of his BMW X5 for Danny to get in, then climbed into the front passenger seat while Wade drove.

'Where are we going?' Danny demanded.

'New Scotland Yard,' Cain answered without looking back at Danny.

As they drove through the London suburbs, Danny's senses put him on high alert. Wade kept giving him sideways glances in the rear view mirror, and Cain shuffled nervously around in his seat. Another fifteen minutes passed and Danny noticed they were heading away from central London towards Romford, and not towards New Scotland Yard.

'So where are we really going?' Danny said calmly.

Cain turned around in the front seat to face Danny, a Glock 17 pistol appearing around the side of the seat. 'Just sit back, Pearson, it won't be long now,' Cain said.

'Where's Delany?' Danny said, not moving. He looked

relaxed, but under his clothes every muscle in his body was tense and ready to move.

'That's not something you have to concern yourself with,' Cain answered.

Danny's eyes narrowed as he looked defiantly at Cain. In his peripheral vision, he watched the road up ahead and Wade's eyes in the rear view mirror. They drove on in silence for another five minutes. Wade indicated off the A12 and slowed to take the turn. As they rounded the corner, Cain's eyes flicked away from Danny for a second, the natural urge to see where they were going too great for him to resist. Time slowed as Danny released every ounce of tensed up energy, launching forward to grab the barrel of the Glock in his left hand. He wrenched the gun sideways behind the front seat, so it pointed away from him. As it ripped from Cain's hand, his finger pulled back on the trigger. The shot was deafening in the enclosed space. The bullet punched through the rear passenger window, leaving it crystallised but intact for a split second before the glass lost its surface tension and disintegrated in a million shiny crystals.

Before the fragments hit the seat, Danny powered his right fist into Cain's face, knocking him to the dashboard at the front of the car. Deafened and confused, Wade started braking. Still gripping the barrel of the Glock, Danny whipped it across and smashed the back of the slide into Wade's temple, repeating the blow over and over until Wade's head flopped to one side. The car veered across the oncoming traffic, bumping up the kerb to the sound of horns before crashing into a railing-topped wall. Danny crunched into the back of the front passenger seat while Wade and Cain disappeared inside the exploding airbags in the front.

Pushing the door open, Danny half climbed, half fell out of the back of the car. A cloud of smoke from the explosive charges in the airbags wafted out of the car as he steadied himself on his feet. When he staggered to the front of the car, it took a couple of seconds to take in the damage. The car had punched through the low wall, forcing the bottom of the railings forward as it went. The railings twisted downwards until their spiked tops punched through the windscreen and Wade's chest until they burst through the back into the driver's seat. Still twisted to face Danny, Cain never saw them coming. The spikes entered his back, pinning him to the front seat, his face staring lifelessly at the back seat.

Fuck.

A scream and crying from behind him shook him into action. He turned to see two women step out of their car, staring at Cain and Wade in shock. Danny walked past them as one stared at the car and the other called 999 with shaky hands. He pushed the passenger door of their still running car shut before moving swiftly around to the driver's side to get in. Before they realised what was happening, Danny threw the car into gear and screamed off up the road, turning back onto the A12 to head back towards central London and Scott's flat.

CHAPTER 44

Delany glanced up at the "Oyster Catchers" name plaque as they arrived at the house on Mersea Island. Tyson and Billy pulled up on the drive seconds after he got out of the car. The house was on Mersea Island's coast road, with panoramic views of the West Mersea Marine boatyard and the mouth of the river Blackwater as it opened out to the North Sea. Delany went inside, heading straight upstairs to the master bedroom with his phone glued to his ear. He looked out the bifold doors past the glass and steel veranda to the sea. Downstairs, Ken, Tyson and Billy searched the empty kitchen for something to make a brew. Hopkins sat at the table, nervously looking at the words *"Access denied, please contact the bank"* displayed on the laptop screen as another account got hit by the authorities seizing Delany's assets. He'd moved millions of pounds to Delany's Cayman Islands accounts before getting locked out of the last of the holding accounts, and was now melting into a nervous wreck at the thought of having to tell Mr Delany he couldn't move any more. Delany came back downstairs, his face like thunder as he walked past Hopkins into the kitchen.

'Tyson, go into the town and get some food and a bottle of good Scotch,' he said, handing Tyson a wedge of notes.

'Yes boss,' Tyson said, taking the money and heading out the door to the car.

Delany's phone rang as Tyson's headlights disappeared up the road.

'Yes, what? They've arrested Jake? Shit. No, no, he's a good lad, he won't talk. Look, keep the pickups as normal. I'm going to send two guys down to take Jake's place.'

Delany hung up and walked back into the living room, still in a bad mood. He glanced over at Hopkins as he scrolled through his contacts deciding who else he needed to call. He stopped mid-scroll, noticing the trickle of sweat rolling down Hopkins' face while he sat not tapping at the keyboard of his laptop.

'Talk,' he demanded.

'I can't do any more, Mr Delany. The authorities have seized all your accounts,' Hopkins said, barely able to look Delany in the eye.

'You moved the money, right?' Delany barked at him.

'Some of it,' Hopkins stuttered.

'How much?' Delany shouted, the veins on his temple and neck rising as his face went red.

'I, I managed to move two and a half million into your Cayman Islands accounts before they shut me down.'

'What? Fuck, what about the rest? What about the other five? Fuck, fuck, fuck. That's not enough to keep the supply chain going. I need more,' Delany growled, pacing up and down the living room.

'I'm sorry, Mr Delany. There's nothing more I can do.'

'You're sorry, you're fucking sorry. All this is your fault.

If you hadn't left that memory stick unattended, none of this would have happened.'

'I, I—'

Before Hopkins could get his words out, Delany grabbed the end of the table and hurled it and the laptop out of the way in a rage. As Hopkins raised his hand in defence, Delany grabbed one of the other chairs in both hands, swinging it up in the air before smashing it down into Hopkins' head. The blow knocked Hopkins backwards off his chair to land flat on his back. Enraged, Delany kept smashing the chair on Hopkins until the legs splintered off and it disintegrated into pieces. Coughing and spitting blood, Hopkins raised his arms in a feeble defence.

'You're fucking sorry now, aren't you?' Delany yelled, thumping his knee into Hopkins' chest before driving the jagged, splintered chair leg into his neck.

A gurgling, choking sound emanated from Hopkins' throat as he stared at Delany, his eyes wide with panic. He trembled and coughed blood while a pool of the sticky red fluid spread around his head. After a few seconds he went silent. His eyes lost their shine, becoming dull and lifeless.

When Delany got up, Ken and Billy were watching from the kitchen door, Ken's face giving a look of emotional indifference while Billy tried to disguise his shock at his boss's violent outburst.

'Put him in the garage. You and Tyson can get rid of him on your way back to London,' Delany said, breathing heavily as he walked out of the room. 'And clean that shit up,' he yelled as he headed up the stairs.

'Yes boss,' Billy said while Ken headed casually into the kitchen to grab a roll of bin bags and tape to wrap the body up in.

Upstairs, Delany headed into the ensuite bathroom and washed the blood off his hands before unbuttoning his blood splattered shirt. His phone rang with Samuel Mendez's number as he pulled on a clean shirt.

'Talk to me, Samuel,' Delany barked down the phone.

'We're OK. We got every shipment out and we washed the back room out with chlorine and beach before the Civil Guard and Interpol turned up. They left with no proof.'

'Good, good, and the lorry?'

'He's just boarded the ferry at Calais. Once he has dropped off the shipment, he will pick you up and drive you back here. I will arrange with our Algerian smuggler, Nazim, to have his yacht take you to Béjaïa, Algeria. Carlos Kraymar will fly you into the Sudan from there.'

'Thank you, my friend, but we have another problem to sort out before I go,' Delany said, his voice a little calmer.

'What sort of problem?' Mendez said cautiously.

'The authorities froze my assets before I could get all my money out. I haven't got enough to pay the Sudanese for the next shipment.'

'How much are you short?'

'I need another one and a half mill.'

'Mmm, it'll be tight but I should be able to get it. I will need a fast return, though. Your distribution network is still intact?'

'The dealer network is safe. Our dealers weren't mentioned on the memory stick, it was only the supply chain and financial details on the memory stick.'

'Ok, good. I will see you in a few days,' said Mendez.

'Yes, you will. This is just a temporary setback, Samuel. We'll make some adjustments and then it's business as usual,' Delany said, before hanging up.

He finished buttoning up his clean shirt and then wrote a list of contact names and addresses before going downstairs. In the kitchen, Tyson was putting the groceries away while Ken made a brew.

'Tea, boss?' Ken asked.

'Thanks, Ken,' Delany replied, before turning to Billy and Tyson. 'There's been a change of plan. Once you two have drunk that, I want you to head back to London. Here's a list of names, contacts and addresses. Follow the list in order, phone them when you're there and they'll give you the takings. Let them know nothing has changed, ok. If any of them step out of line, you give them a slap, right? You make sure they know that if they cross me, I'll fucking bury them.'

'Yes boss,' Billy and Tyson said in unison.

'Good, come back here with the cash when you've finished. I'm going to see Mendez in Spain before I head over to see the Sudanese suppliers. Ken will be in charge while I'm gone. You do exactly as he says, you understand?'

'Yes boss.'

CHAPTER 45

'Come on, open the door,' said Danny, buzzing Scott's second apartment from the entry door.

'Who is it?' came Fergus's voice over the door entry intercom.

'Just open the door, dickhead, I'm not in the mood.'

'Alright, keep your hair on,' grumbled Fergus, the lock buzzing a second later.

Moving past the lifts, Danny took the stairs two at a time, all the way up to the fourth floor. He pushed through the fire door into the corridor and walked past Chaz as he held the door to Scott's apartment open for him.

'Are you alright, old man? You look like you've just run a marathon,' said Scott, showing off the expensive coffee machine built into the apartment's bespoke hand-built kitchen.

'No, Scott, actually, I'm not fucking alright. Thanks to your little stunt with Gregory Delany's memory stick, I've been attacked by a bunch of hormonal teenagers with zombie knives and very nearly got killed by two bent coppers. On top of that, I've got a price on my head which every low down piece of street scum is trying to cash in on.'

'Well don't blame me, dear boy. I was kidnapped at the time, expecting to be killed at any moment. Press that one,' Scott said, turning away from Danny to show Fergus the milk frother.

'And you didn't think of sharing that little nugget of information before now?' Danny growled back, his face like thunder.

'For your information, I tried to tell you several times and you shut me down every time. Maybe if you opened your ears once in a while instead of flexing your muscles, you'd get the full picture. Now, would you like a coffee?' Scott said, while Fergus and Chaz looked between the two of them, ready to cut in if Danny decided to kill Scott.

Danny didn't move for a minute, his mind ticking back over the last few days until he recalled Scott trying to tell him something about the memory stick, and him telling Scott he didn't want to hear it. He finally relaxed and took a seat at the dining table.

'You're right, Scott, I should have listened,' he said apologetically.

'Think nothing of it, dear boy. Here, try this. It's made with Molokai coffee beans from Hawaii,' Scott said, handing Danny a cup topped with frothy milk with a big grin on his face.

Danny looked up at Scott, unable to stop a smile forming on his face. No matter what happened, he couldn't stay mad at his oldest friend for long.

'Chaz, did you get hold of the sisters?' Danny said, turning to Chaz.

'No, both phone numbers are dead. I swung by the address she gave me. The place was empty with a to let sign out front. I think they've moved on. Shame, I really fancied Sandra.'

'Probably for the best. They should be safe. When I questioned the kid that attacked me, he said Delany had only put a price on my head and not any of yours,' said Danny.

'So what's the plan?' Fergus said, taking a seat while putting his coffee and a loaded Glock onto the dining table in front of him.

'Do you mind? You'll scratch the French polish,' Scott said, moving across from the kitchen with placemats, dealing them out before picking Fergus's gun up in disgust between his thumb and forefinger to put it on the placemat. 'I'm surrounded by cavemen,' he said, walking off muttering to himself.

Danny pulled Cain's gun from his jacket and placed it on the mat while Chaz slid a Glock from a shoulder holster and put it down on the placemat.

'So how do we find Delany?' said Chaz.

'We start with one of his dealers, a guy named Lionel who works out of the Hazlewood estate. If he doesn't know, we work our way up the chain until we find someone who does,' Danny said, taking the magazine out of his gun before sliding the bullets out one at a time to count them.

'Excellent plan. When do we depart?' came Scott's voice from the kitchen.

'I admire your enthusiasm, Scotty boy, but I think you ought to let us deal with this,' said Danny.

'I beg to differ. Seeing as I might have inadvertently caused this present situation, I feel I should have some involvement in the solution to the problem,' said Scott, sitting down at the table before pulling out a round, barrelled object with two metal prongs protruding from the top.

'What the fuck's that?' said Fergus, frowning.

'It's a stun gun, European model, very powerful, and totally illegal in the UK,' said Scott with a naughty schoolboy smile, clicking the trigger so a blue spark cracked between the metal prongs.

'Ok, ok, you can come, but you do as I say, no heroics, you hear me?' said Danny, rolling his eyes at the stun gun.

'Absolutely. Perhaps I can be the driver.'

'Perfect. And Scott?'

'Yes.'

'Don't put that in your trouser pocket, you're liable to burn your bollocks off.'

CHAPTER 46

After they deliberated over which of Scott's seven cars was the best to take, they headed out of the underground car park in the Audi RS5. They made a stop on the way back to Walthamstow, ducking into an outdoor clothing shop to get strange looks from the woman on the till as she rang through four hooded jackets, gaffer tape and four balaclavas.

'Thank you very much, my dear,' Scott said politely, taking the receipt off her.

Danny, Fergus and Chaz stood behind him looking like they were going straight from the store to rob the nearest bank. They continued on their way, arriving at the Hazelwood estate as the sun was setting.

'Pull in over there, Scott.' Danny said, pointing to a space on the road that gave them a view into the estate made up of four, three-storey blocks of flats set in a square around a green and playground.

'You see him?' Fergus asked, staring through the gap between the corner of two blocks at a couple of youths sitting on the swings in the playground.

'Not yet, but there's a kid coming in from the far corner on an e-bike, looks like one of his gang.'

They watched the kid as he rode his bike over to the youths on the swings. He said something to one of them, triggering him to pull a phone out of his pocket. The youth tapped on the screen to send a message before saying something back to the kid. The kid turned and rode towards Danny and the others in the car. He stopped in the road a little way behind them. As they watched, another kid on an e-bike appeared from between the houses opposite. He rode over and handed him a small package before heading back the way he came. The first kid pocketed the package and rode off. A few minutes later they watched him return to the youth on the swings and hand him what looked like a roll of cash.

'Slick operation, they never keep the cash and drugs in one place,' Chaz said.

'Yeah, but at some point, the big man's going to turn up for the takings,' Danny said.

'Lionel?'

'Yeah, Lionel,' Danny said, his eyes watching a car pull in a little way up the road.

The window lowered and the man inside beckoned one of Lionel's runners over. The kid took the order then rode over to the youth on the swings. He text a number as the kid rode off and the package drop and cash transfer happened all over again. Over the next two hours, they watched this repeatedly, with no sign of Lionel. Finally, at around 10 p.m. the youth holding all the cash on the swing got a call on his phone. He answered it, listening for only a few seconds before hanging up and getting to his feet. He said a few words to the youth beside him. They fist bumped and he left, heading across the green to the far side of the estate.

'Scott, drive us down the side of the estate,' said Danny, his eyes never leaving the youth.

'Absolutely,' Scott said, pulling out of the parking space to take a left down the side of the next block of flats.

'Take it slow,' said Danny, his eyes searching for the youth as he walked out from between the two buildings. 'There he is, and that's Lionel. Pull over here.'

Lionel was standing up ahead, no e-bike, helmet or balaclava this time, just a street hardened kid looking back and forth, his untrusting eyes constantly darting around his surroundings. His dreadlocks spun as he turned his head to look at the approaching youth. They fist bumped, then stood apart. There was a mutual scan of their surroundings before the youth pulled a fat roll of notes out of his pocket and passed them to Lionel, who pocketed them immediately.

'Get ready, boys. As soon as they part, we'll grab Lionel and shove him in the boot. We can take him to your uncle's derelict factory, Chaz,' said Danny, pulling the balaclava down over his face.

Fergus, Chaz and Scott did the same, all four of them watching Lionel closely.

'Here we go,' Danny said, prompting Scott to start the engine, ready to move.

The youth left Lionel and headed back towards the playground. Lionel turned and walked a couple of paces before stopping to answer his phone.

'Hang on a minute,' Danny said to Scott.

Putting it to his ear, Lionel turned his head to look down the road past Danny and the others in the car. Seconds later a BMW X7 came past them and pulled up beside Lionel. The window came down and Tyson's hand reached out from within the car.

'Who the fuck are these guys?' said Fergus, pulling up the balaclava.

'They're the next step up the food chain and more likely to know where Delany is,' said Danny, taking off his balaclava along with Chaz.

They watched as Lionel handed over the cash. The driver passed it over to a man in the passenger seat before turning back to him. He was talking at Lionel rather than to him, his finger stabbing in Lionel's direction like a knife. Lionel's face looked worried and he was shaking his head and talking fast as if he was trying to convince the driver of something. The discussion seemed to come to some sort of conclusion because Lionel stepped back from the car and the window went up.

'Follow that car, Scott, but not too close, mate,' Danny said.

'Roger that,' said Scott excitedly, driving after the BMW while grinning like a big kid with the balaclava still on his head.

'You can take that off now,' Fergus said, reaching over from behind Scott to whip the balaclava off his head.

'Oh, yes, quite. I got a bit carried away with all the excitement,' Scott said, gripping the steering wheel tightly.

'All right, Scotty boy, just breathe, mate, take it easy, yeah.' Danny said, watching the BMW up ahead.

CHAPTER 47

With Scott driving, Danny and the others moved from one London suburb to another, keeping well back from Tyson and Billy as they collected money from one dealer to another.

'We're going to have to take them soon,' Chaz said from the back of the Audi RS5.

'Agreed. We'll move as soon as they are away from this housing estate. Same deal as we were planning for Lionel. Balaclavas to make them think we're a rival outfit. Me and Ferg will take them at gunpoint, tape them up, put them in their boot, then drive them to the derelict factory in their car. You and Scott follow behind, ok?' Danny said, pulling his balaclava over his head as the BMW X7 left the dealer and drove away from the estate.

'I say, chaps, you'll have to smash the windows to get in, the X7's doors auto lock as soon as it gets over ten miles an hour, and don't unlock until the occupants pulls the door release from the inside or turns the engine off,' Scott said, driving off to follow the other car before he could get the balaclava on straight, with the mouth hole over his cheek and his right eye looking out the left eye hole. 'Er, would someone mind?'

'Good shout, Scotty boy, here,' Danny replied, leaning over to give Scott's balaclava a quick twist to set it straight.

'Ah, that's much better,' Scott said, grinning.

They drove on for a few more streets, all eyes glued to the back of the BMW through the holes in their balaclavas. The traffic lights at roadworks up ahead turned red, causing the BMW to stop closely behind a taxi cab.

'Now, Scott, get up close behind them, sandwich them in,' Danny said, his hand on the door release handle, ready to leap out.

Scott did as Danny said, pulling up close to the other car's bumper. The second he'd stopped, Danny and Fergus slid out from each side of the car and moved forward in a low crouch. They arrived on either side of the front doors in unison, swinging their arms back before striking the tempered glass with the butt of their handguns.

The implosion of glass crystals made Billy and Tyson jump. Danny and Fergus shoved the barrel of their guns inches away from Billy and Tyson's faces, while reaching inside with their other hand to pull the door release handle before Billy and Tyson had time to react.

'Keep your hands where we can see them,' Danny said in a gruff voice, punching the ignition button to kill the engine before sliding his hand inside Tyson's jacket to pull his gun from its shoulder holster.

Fergus took Billy's gun on the opposite side of the car and dragged him out of the vehicle, slamming him against its side while pulling his hands behind his back to gaffer tape them together.

'Do you know who we work for? If you rob us, you're signing your own death warrant,' Tyson said calmly as

Danny shoved him up against the car and taped his hands behind his back.

'Rob you? Wow, I hadn't thought of that. Thanks, that's a great idea,' Danny said, spinning the tape around Tyson's ankles before patting his pockets to find the car's key fob. He pressed the boot open button then spun Tyson around and picked him up over his shoulder.

He met Fergus with Billy over his shoulder at the boot, the two of them dumping Tyson and Billy inside.

'Sit tight, boys,' said Fergus, slapping tape across their mouths before shutting the boot.

The driver of the van in front suddenly sped off, too scared to get involved, he jumped the lights after seeing Danny with a gun carrying Tyson to the rear of the vehicle, all taped up.

Fergus and Danny jumped back into the BMW and drove away, with Scott and Chaz following closely behind. They removed their balaclavas and drove like they were on their driving test, heading away from central London.

'Fuck me, have you seen this lot?' Fergus said, pulling a sports bag from the back seat and unzipping to find it stuffed with fat rolls of cash held together with elastic bands.

'We'll divide it up once we've taken care of Delany, mate. Can't spend it if we're all dead,' Danny said without taking his eyes off the road.

'I'm with you on that one,' replied Fergus, zipping the bag back up.

After twenty minutes, they entered the derelict factory, with the noise of traffic from the M25 motorway rumbling through the trees and a thick hedgerow to its rear.

They drove in through a loading bay with a missing

roller door and parked side by side so the bright lights of the cars beamed across the empty factory floor.

'Here, point this and look mean,' Danny said, handing Scott the gun he'd taken off Tyson, checking that the safety was on first.

'Like this?' Scott said, narrowing his eyes and baring his teeth through the balaclava.

'Perfect, mate,' chuckled Danny. 'Right, let's get them out.'

Fergus and Chaz dragged Tyson and Billy out of the boot, pushing them down on their knees in front of the cars before standing behind them with the barrel of their guns on the backs of Tyson and Billy's heads. With the headlights blinding Tyson and Billy, all they could see were Danny and Scott's outline. Danny nodded to Fergus and Chaz, who reached forward and ripped the tape off Tyson and Billy's mouths.

'You fucking lot are dead men walking, you hear me? Dead men. We work for Gregory Delany, you understand? There's nowhere you can go, nowhere you can hide that he won't find you,' spat Tyson, his face screwed up in a defiant snarl.

'Oh, we're not hiding from him, pal. We want to know where he is, and you're going to tell us,' Danny said, squatting down in front of Tyson so he could see his eyes as he spoke.

'Fuck off,' Tyson spat back.

Danny stood up and stepped back, falling into a featureless black outline against the car headlights. He stood quietly, studying the two men in front of him. The SAS had taught him interrogation techniques, including methods that he, Fergus, and Chaz would never speak about to anyone outside the regiment. Tyson was tough, a loyal foot soldier to Delany. He would talk, everybody talks eventually, but it was going to take a lot of beating and torture, and time, before he gave anything up. Billy, however, was different. The fear and panic in his face bled through his poor attempt at looking defiant. Billy was the weak link. Danny nodded to Fergus, who immediately moved in behind Tyson. He swung his arm around Tyson's neck, pulling it into a choke hold with his other hand. Danny darted forward, kicking Tyson in the balls as hard as he could, making Billy flinch beside him. A second later, Fergus released him to fall forward onto his front, coughing, grunting and gasping in agony.

'Where's Delany?' Danny growled, squatting down to grab Tyson by the hair, pulling his face up to look at him.

Tyson gasped several times before managing to grunt, 'Fuck off.'

As he got the last word out, Danny smashed his fist into Tyson's face so hard his head thumped down onto the concrete floor, leaving Danny's other hand suspended in midair with a clump of Tyson's hair still hanging from his clenched fist.

'Kill him,' Danny said to Fergus, who dragged Tyson's semi-conscious body back away from them.

Billy tried to look round, only to get a smack around the back of the head from Chaz's gun, making him face forward nervously. The deafening sound of a gunshot rang out a second later, making Billy jump out of his skin, the last remnants of courage leaving his body as he started shaking and snivelling. Tears trickled down his cheeks.

'Last chance, dickhead. Tell me where Delany is or you can join your mate,' Danny said, moving in close to Billy's face.

'Mersea Island. He's at a house on Mersea Island,' Billy said with a shaky voice.

'Where on Mersea Island?' Danny shouted in his face.

'I, I, it was called the Oyster Catcher. It's on the coast road opposite the West Mersea Marine boatyard,' Billy sobbed.

'How many guys has he got with him? Answer me,' Danny said with Chaz racking the slide back on his handgun behind Billy's head for added effect.

'No, please, just Ken, Kenneth Gambit, his right-hand man. Delany's heading to Spain to see Samuel Mendez before he goes to Africa.'

'How is he getting to Spain?' Danny shouted at him.

'I don't know, I swear I don't know,' Billy yelled before sobbing uncontrollably.

'Good lad,' Danny said, removing the balaclava to give Billy a grin.

Scott removed his balaclava while Chaz stepped in behind Billy and turned him around so he could see Fergus pinning Tyson to the ground a few metres away, gaffer tape over his mouth so he couldn't make a sound, his eyes staring at Billy in disgust at his weakness.

After manhandling the two men into the boot of Scott's Audi, Danny, Scott, Chaz and Fergus got back in the car with the bag of money before Scott circled back out of the factory.

CHAPTER 48

elany poured himself another glass of Glenfiddich 15 year old Scotch whisky and sat back in the chair on the glass and steel terrace off the master bedroom. He looked out over the moonlit estuary with unseeing eyes, the turmoil spinning around in his head hiding the beauty of the view in front of him. With his business in tatters and his face distributed across every law enforcement agency in the country, most men would have resigned to their fate and mentally prepared themselves for life in jail. Gregory Delany wasn't most men. He sipped the whisky and called DCI Cain for the third time, only to get his voicemail for the third time. Annoyed, Delany slammed the phone down on the table in front of him without leaving a message.

'Everything alright, boss?' came Ken's voice from the driveway below.

Delany sat up and looked over to see Ken finish a cigarette and stamp it out on the tarmac.

'Fucking Cain's gone AWOL. If that bastard's trying to

screw me over, I'll tear him apart,' Delany said, standing up with his hands on the stainless steel railing across the top of the glass balustrade.

'Cain's a lot of things, boss, but he's no grass. I'll call Tyson and Billy, get them to swing by Cain's apartment on the way back.'

'Good idea, thanks, Ken.'

Ken got straight on the phone, pacing up and down the driveway while it rang without being answered, eventually going to Tyson's voicemail. Delany caught Ken's frown as he watched him from above. Ken called Tyson again, listening to it ring until it went to voicemail as before.

'I'll try Billy's phone,' Ken said, looking up at Delany, his usual unreadable face showing slight signs of apprehension.

The call went the same way as Tyson's, leaving Ken frowning at the phone. 'There's no answer.'

Delany turned his head away from Ken, narrowing his eyes as he scanned his surroundings for the trouble he felt was heading his way. When nothing presented itself, he looked back down at Ken.

'Call the dealers. I want to know who saw them last,' Delany said, heading inside and down the stairs to meet Ken as he came into the kitchen, the phone glued to his ear.

'They picked up from Merrick's crew a couple of hours ago,' Ken said, hanging up and calling the next dealer.

He repeated the process four more times, tracking Tyson and Billy's pickups across London while Delany paced around the kitchen, his head turning in Ken's direction every time he heard him speak to another dealer.

'Dex, it's Ken. What time did Tyson and Billy do the pickup?'

'Ken, man, I waited for an hour. They're a no show, geez. Is it true what I hear about the boss man, that the filth has got his number, eh? Should we be worried, man?'

Catching bits of the conversation, Delany snatched the phone off Ken and yelled at Dex, 'Nothing's changed. I'm still running the show, you hear me? Just do your fucking job, Dexter. Don't make me replace you.'

'Whoa, sorry, Mr Delany, I meant no disrespect, man. I was just saying, there are a lot of rumours flying around and I just heard the terminator guy killed your detective man. He crashed their car and shish kebabbed them on some railings. Proper mess, man.'

'What terminator guy? What the fuck are you talking about?' Delany growled, annoyed by Dex's waffling.

'The guy, you know, the guy. The guy you put the hit out on. They're saying you just can't kill the dude. He took out half of Lionel's crew earlier today, single-handed, man.'

Delany thrust the phone back to Ken, his face going bright red as it contorted with rage. 'Fucking Pearson,' he yelled, launching his whisky glass into the sink, where it exploded into flying shards of glass.

'Fuck off, Dex, I'll arrange a new pickup tomorrow,' Ken said, hanging up.

Still enraged, Delany picked up the stool from the breakfast bar and smashed it repeatedly onto the marble worktop until it disintegrated into flying legs and snapped foot bars and a foam seat.

Ken stood back and watched, waiting for Delany to run out of steam and calm down. He eventually just stood still, panting, his mind spinning over what Dex had said.

'Phone Mendez, Ken. Find out where that fucking lorry is now. Right now.'

'What about Tyson and Billy?'

'Forget them. They're gone. Just find out where that fucking lorry is. I don't think we're safe here.'

'Yes boss.'

CHAPTER 49

Leaving Colchester behind, Scott flew through sleeping villages with only the occasional car to overtake as he headed east towards Mersea Island. The villages gave way to fields, then marshland as they approached the causeway onto the island. Scott sped on with spray hitting the windows as he ploughed through a couple of inches of seawater, still on the causeway from the recently turned high tide. With a clear night sky and bright full moon, the estuary and island ahead lit up in clear monotone detail, almost as sharp as its day time equivalent.

'I wish it was cloudier,' said Chaz, looking across the shimmering water.

'Yeah, me too,' said Fergus.

They continued up into the old fishing town of West Mersea, its pubs, shops and restaurants all dark and empty at half two in the morning. The road dipped sharply as it exited the high street and dropped onto the coast road, with big houses on the right and views out over the estuary to the left.

'Drive past the house slowly, Scott,' Danny said, as the West Mersea Marina boatyard came into view up ahead.

All eyes looked left, taking in Delany's house on the incline above them. A light was on in the master bedroom and another inside the house on the ground floor.

'Park it up over there,' Danny said to Scott when they were safely past the boatyard.

'How do you want to play it?' said Chaz, checking his weapon.

'Yes, how do you want to play it, old man?' chipped in Scott through a yawn.

'Ok, Rambo, I think we'll take it from here. You just sit tight and look after the two in the boot,' Danny said, unable to help himself from grinning at Scott.

'Please yourselves, I know when I'm not wanted,' Scott said with a hurt look on his face.

'Well, if you really want to come and watch me blow Delany's brains out all over the floor, Scotty boy, feel free.'

'Mmm, on second thoughts, perhaps not. I'll just sit tight and babysit our friends in the boot,' Scott said.

'Right, Ferg, you give Chaz a leg up to the terrace, then head around the rear of the house. Chaz, you go in through the bedroom. Fergus, you go in through the back, I'll take the side door. The hired muscle in the back says there's only Delany and this other bloke there, but we'll work on the assumption that there might be more,' Danny said, opening the car door.

'Roger that. Let's get this done so we can all go home,' said Fergus, stepping out of the car to muffled thumps coming from the boot.

Chaz stepped forward and opened it with Danny on the right and Fergus on the left pointing their guns at

STEPHEN TAYLOR

Tyson and Billy as they fought against their taped up limbs, trying to get free.

'If I hear any more out of you two, I'm going to shoot a bunch of air holes into this boot and I don't care what they hit on the inside, do you understand me?' Danny growled, before slamming the boot shut to silence.

Crouching behind a low perimeter wall belonging to the neighbouring property, the three of them moved along the road towards Delany's house. Flattening himself against the end of the wall, Danny pushed his head out until one eye looked past the corner towards Delany's house at the top of the drive. The lights were still on behind the blinds, but he couldn't see anybody looking out, or any shadowy outlines from anyone within. Without taking his eye off the house, he moved a hand behind him and waved Chaz and Fergus to go. He watched them run up the drive ahead of him, Fergus turning ahead of Chaz to flatten his back against the front wall of the house. He placed his gun on the floor, bent his legs slightly, and linked his fingers. A second later, Chaz placed his foot in Fergus's hands and reached up for the terrace railing in front of the master bedroom. Fergus kept pushing him upwards until Chaz could grab the railing and pull himself over.

At the same time, Danny moved past Fergus and flattened himself against the wall by the side entrance into the house. He waited until Fergus picked his gun up and ran past him, disappearing out of sight around the back of the house. Taking a count of ten, Danny pictured Chaz entering the master bedroom as Fergus entered from the rear of the property. On ten he tried the side door. Thankfully, it was unlocked, allowing him to ease it silently open and slide through into a utility room. Moving to the next

206

door, which he presumed led to the kitchen beyond, Danny held his gun up ready while turning the door handle until the latch had withdrawn far enough for the door to be pushed open. On the count of three, he burst through the door at the same time Fergus rushed in to his left and Chaz swung his gun into view from the stairs on the far side of the kitchen. Danny trained his gun on the figure sitting at the kitchen table, his finger tensing on the trigger before backing off when the figure's features registered in his brain.

'Congratulations gentlemen, a textbook entry. Now if you wouldn't mind lowering your unlicensed, illegal firearms. One wouldn't want you to hurt oneself, would one?' said the government man known only as Simon, sitting with his legs crossed and relaxed at the table with a steaming hot cup of tea in front of him.

'Simon, what the fuck are you doing here?' Danny said, without hiding his contempt for the man who'd constantly managed to intrude on his life.

Before Simon could answer, there was noise and movement from every direction. Danny, Chaz and Fergus spun around with guns up, only to be faced by a special operations team in full tactical kit pointing C8 carbine rifles at them, an array of little red laser target dots dancing around on Danny, Chaz and Fergus's chests.

'I, Daniel, am trying to apprehend one Gregory Delany, but as you can see, he would appear to have left before we got here. What I think is the vastly more important question is what you and, er, your friends are doing here?' said Simon, before turning to one of the special operations force. ' You can stand down now, Staff Sergeant, we're all friends here,' Simon continued with a slight upper hand smile on his face.

Danny shot him a look, the muscles in his jaw flexing and eyes burning murderously.

As the dots dropped from their chests and the men backed away, the sound of Scott's protesting voice came from outside.

'Do you mind? Unhand me, you oaf. I have my rights.'

Two soldiers marched him into the kitchen, with Tyson and Billy being escorted behind him.

'Those two are Delany's. Would you mind popping them in the van and giving us some privacy? Thank you,' Simon asked the staff sergeant in charge of the unit.

'Yes sir,' he replied, jerking his head for the men to disperse, which they did, moving out of the house in record time.

'Now, gentlemen, I asked you a question. Oh, hang on a minute. I should have known. The reports of English mercenaries in ridiculous clothing waging war against Spanish gangsters. The destruction of half of Benidorm, and the sophisticated upload of all Mr Delany's business affairs. This has yours and Mr Miller's names written all over it. Mmm, I can tell I'm right by the looks on your faces. So, do tell, what is your involvement with Gregory Delany?' Simon finished, picking up his tea to take a sip while he waited for an answer.

CHAPTER 50

Ken took the slip road off the M25 and followed the one way approach road around the outside of Thurrock services, passing the lorry park and rows of lorries with curtains drawn around the cabs as the drivers slept in bunks behind the driver's seats. An early morning mist floated across the service area, giving an eerie dystopian look as they entered the nearly empty car park at the far side of the services.

'Is he here yet?' Ken asked, pulling the vehicle to a stop near the entrance to the services.

'No, we've got about twenty minutes. Come on, I need a coffee, the whisky's wearing off,' Delany said, rubbing his face to wake himself up.

After grabbing the sports bag full of money and papers and his gun, the two of them walked towards the services, trying to look as relaxed as possible. Their eyes flicked around as they entered, paranoia causing them to expect the police to storm in at any minute. They moved over to the 24-hour Costa Coffee and ordered two coffees from a young man with dark rings under his eyes and zero interest in the two men ordering on the other side of the counter. They took their drinks and sat in Costa's seating area along with only one other customer, a middle-aged guy in grimy overalls sitting in the corner, staring at social media posts on his phone. Ken sipped his drink while watching every blurry eyed, early morning traveller that entered and left the services, while Delany sat opposite finishing a call.

'Any news on Tyson and Billy?'

'Nothing, the police haven't got them. If they've done a runner with my money, I'll fucking kill them,' Delany said gruffly.

'They wouldn't, boss, Tyson and Billy are solid. Besides, the pickup money wasn't enough to disappear on. Nah, something's happened to them, I can feel it,' Ken said, his voice calm and collected as always.

'I'm leaving you in charge, Ken, you find out what's happened to Tyson and Billy, and if they - or anyone else - steps out of line, you show no mercy. If those bastards see any weakness, they'll start making a play for control, and I'll have no business to come back to.'

'If you don't mind me asking, how do you intend to come back? The cops have you bang to rights, you'll be picked up the moment you step back into the country.'

Delany leant forward towards Ken and smiled.

'It won't be me coming back. I thought that one day the authorities might get something on me. I've got myself a backup plan. Once I've secured our next load from the Sudanese, I'm flying to Cape Town. I've got a new identity, rock solid, with fingerprint and matching dental records, and a no-questions-asked plastic surgeon on standby to give me a new face. I just need you to take care of things here for a couple of months while my face heals, then I'll be back. You do this for me and I'll make you a very rich man,' Delany said quietly, looking around to make sure they weren't overheard.

An uncharacteristic smile formed on Ken's face. 'Right, boss, you can trust me.'

A ping on Delany's phone took his attention off Ken as he looked at the message.

'He's here,' Delany said, standing up.

The two of them exited the services, turning right to head for the lorry park instead of the car park. A large white DAF lorry with a refrigerated trailer flashed its lights from a parking bay as they approached. Delany walked around to the passenger side and stepped up to open the door. He threw the bag inside before turning back to Ken.

'Get rid of this. I'll buy another burner in Dover and text you the number before we get on the ferry,' Delany said, throwing Ken his mobile.

Ken caught it and nodded. He watched Delany get into the cab. The driver revved the large diesel engine as he drove out of the space and turned onto the exit road, disappearing from view moments later. Ken looked down at Delany's phone, the thought of phoning the police and telling them where Delany was crossing his mind for a fleeting moment. He dismissed it. Even if Delany was in prison and he took over, Delany could still have him killed.

No, do as Delany says and keep everything running smoothly. Or maybe there is another option.

Ken pulled Delany's phone apart on the way back to the car, snapping the SIM card in half before dropping the phone on the floor and stamping on it until it was a shattered, bent-up mess. He picked it up and chucked it into the nearest bin before getting into the car and starting it.

First things first, go home and get some sleep. Second thing, find out where the fuck Tyson and Billy are.

He drove through the mist and exited the services before joining the M25 and heading home.

CHAPTER 51

Danny reluctantly relayed a short version of the events in Benidorm to Simon, with Scott proudly filling in his own overly embellished version of how brilliantly he'd cracked Delany's memory stick and implemented a virus to email out the contents the next time it was used.

'And that's the reason Mr Delany wants Mr Pearson dead, for revenge,' Simon added dryly, once Scott had finished.

'Er, well, er, yes, I suppose so,' Scott muttered, the smug grin at his brilliance dropping like a stone.

'So your rather dramatic entrance tonight was to — what? Ask Mr Delany politely to remove the price on your head?'

Danny's eyes flicked down to his gun and then back up again. 'Something like that,' he said in a low growl.

'Then it would seem we have both had a wasted night,' said Simon, looking at the time on his watch.

'What's your interest in Delany? Terrorism, political agendas and threats to national security are your department, not drug dealers,' Danny said, eyeing Simon with suspicion.

Simon sat back and said nothing for a few seconds, as if mulling over what to disclose and what not to.

'What do you know about the Sudan, Mr Pearson?'

'It's dry, hot, and the fuckers spend most of their time trying to kill each other,' Danny said bluntly.

'Mmm, quite, other than that colourful insight into the affairs of the Sudan, the country has, amongst other things, very large mineral deposits. More specifically, lithium ore, or white gold, as they are now describing it. They've just hit the motherload of the stuff. Now, as you know, the UK is pulling out all the stops to reach carbon zero by 2050. Our government wants to secure an alliance with the Sudanese government to ensure the steady supply of lithium for our increasing demand for electric cars, solar charged domestic battery packs, and all the other modern conveniences its taxpayers enjoy.'

'Sorry, as interesting as this is, what the fuck has this got to do with Gregory fucking Delany?' Danny said, interrupting Simon.

'If you would let me continue, Daniel, I was just about to get to that. Civil war still rages across large parts of the Sudan, and the lithium mines, although in an area controlled by the Sudanese armed forces, are dangerously close to an area controlled by the paramilitary group, the RSF. Now here comes the interesting bit. One of the high-ranking members of the RSF, a Mr Omar Al Nuran, just happens to be Gregory Delany's cocaine supplier. Mr Delany's vast multi-million pound drug network is funding the RSF's war against the government, and in doing so is threatening the UK's alliance with the

Sudanese government, and the future supply of much needed lithium ore.'

'So it's all just about money and power,' said Scott.

'Isn't it always? We donate a hundred million in humanitarian aid, and the Sudanese government gives us priority over the supply of lithium. But first they need to throttle the RSF's funding, so I've been tasked with resolving the situation,' replied Simon matter-of-fact.

'So you're going to kill Delany?' Scott answered.

A small smile crossed Simon's face as he sat back in his chair again and looked across at Danny.

'No Scott, he wants me to do it,' Danny said gruffly.

Simon just smiled.

'What? Why the hell doesn't he do it?' Scott said, glaring at Simon.

'Because now that Delany has left the country and gone to Spain, he needs plausible deniability if it all goes wrong. What if I refuse?' Danny said, looking menacingly at Simon.

'Entirely your choice, dear boy. You are all free to go. Your recent escapades are of no interest to me. As you said, my department is terrorists, political agendas and threats to national security. But as a law-abiding citizen, I will have to inform the Metropolitan Police about the murders of DCI Matthew Cain and Detective Wade, and I will also have to report the unlicensed firearms. That's a minimum five-year stretch for each of you,' Simon said, gesturing to the guns on the table. 'Oh, and Interpol may want to extradite you for questioning about your activities in Benidorm and the death of Alonzo Acosta,' Simon added slowly, his voice neutral as he looked down at his suit trousers and picked a bit of lint off his knee.

A flash of anger crossed Danny's face. He snatched the gun off the table and locked his arm out in front of him, the barrel of the gun pointing squarely between Simon's eyes.

'Danny, mate,' Chaz said, concerned.

'Whoa, come on, mate, don't let him get to you,' said Fergus.

'One might want to listen to one's friends, Daniel. I don't understand what the problem is. After all, you came here tonight to kill Gregory Delany, did you not? Let me help you get your wish and I'll make sure your record is clean, and that you're back from Spain in time for your wedding to that lovely lady friend of yours. Nikki, isn't it?' Simon said, staring past the barrel of the gun to look Danny squarely in the eyes.

Nobody moved for what felt like an eternity. Simon's face flinched as his confidence wavered for a fraction of a second when Danny's finger tensed on the trigger before finally relaxing. Scott, Chaz and Fergus all breathed a sigh of relief as Danny finally placed the gun back on the table.

'Excellent, I'll make flight arrangements.'

'When do we go?' said Fergus.

'The deal is for Mr Pearson only. Mr Leman, Mr Miller and yourself are to leave, now. Oh, and you can leave the firearms with me. One wouldn't want you getting arrested on your way home.'

'No way, you can fuck right off, you bastard,' growled Fergus, kicking the chair out as he stood up, ready to punch Simon in the face.

'Leave it, Ferg, it's ok. I'll take care of this. You guys just go home. I'll see you at the wedding,' Danny said, getting up to push Fergus back from the table.

'But mate,' Chaz said, also getting up.

'No buts, go home, I'll take care of this,' Danny said,

his two friends and Scott eventually relinquishing and heading out of the house, past the special operations team and back down the road to Scott's car.

'You can drop all the coincidence bullshit now. You knew every detail of what happened in Benidorm and what's been happening back here. How come you didn't just kill Delany when he was here?' Danny said when the others had gone.

Simon just gave him a dry smile. 'It's my job to know everything, Daniel, and unfortunately sometimes that knowledge comes to us a little too late. We came as soon as the information about Mr Delany's little holiday home here came into our possession. As I told you earlier, Mr Delany had already vacated the property by the time we got here. Now, we are fairly sure Mr Delany hasn't left the country by air or the Eurostar, which means he's gone by small boat or ferry and then road. We estimate he won't rendezvous with Mr Mendez for at least another sixteen hours. I suggest you make use of the king sized bed upstairs and get some sleep. I'll wake you when it's time to go.'

Danny said nothing. Adrenaline levels were dropping and tiredness was kicking in fast. Reluctantly he walked past Simon and headed upstairs to the master bedroom. Slipping his shoes off, he lay on top of the bed fully clothed and forced himself to clear his mind and go to sleep.

CHAPTER 52

As they approached the Dover ferry terminal, Delany pulled the mattress up on the bunk at the rear of the cab and lifted the lid to a storage compartment underneath. Turning on the torch the driver had given him, he held the lid and mattress up while sliding inside, letting them drop back down as he lay down out of sight. The driver of the lorry entered the port, looking bored as he passed his passport over to the tired-looking customs officer in the booth at the entrance. He barely looked at it before handing it back and waving the driver on. The lorry had no cargo and nobody smuggled people out of the UK, so the chances of a search were virtually zero.

After being guided into their parking place on the ferry, the driver let Delany out. They sat in the restaurant, Delany drinking coffee with a new burner phone he'd bought at Dover services glued to his ear. The driver sat in silence, watching the sun come up over the Channel. As they approached the port of Calais, the two of them headed back to the lorry, where Delany returned to the storage compartment. The lorry rumbled down off the ferry ramp and through customs with the same ease as it had in Dover, Calais officials using the majority of their resources to check for illegal immigrants and goods being smuggled into the UK, not out. He let Delany out once they cleared the port, driving a further twenty minutes before the driver took the slip road into a large service area just off the motorway.

'Why are we stopping?' Delany said, impatient to keep going.

The driver shrugged, his understanding of English limited. He parked the lorry and pointed at some cars parked across from them.

'You go, *Señor*,' he said, pointing.

Delany looked in the direction he was pointing to see Arlo and Javier standing by a sleek looking Mercedes AMG C63 sports saloon. Understanding, Delany grabbed his bag and climbed down from the cab, crossing the car park towards them.

'Mr Delany, good to see you. Mr Mendez thought this would be more fitting for the rest of the journey. Also, with the two of us taking turns to drive, we can get you to Benidorm faster,' said Arlo, opening the back door for him.

'Good, let's get going,' was all Delany said.

'Lie back and get some rest, Mr Delany. It's a long drive,' said Javier, getting in the driver's seat to take up the first leg of the drive.

As they drove out of the services, Delany lay across the back seat and went to sleep, using his bag as a pillow. Sitting in the passenger seat, Arlo tapped out a message and sent it to Mendez.

"Picked up package safe and sound. We will be back around midnight tonight."

CHAPTER 53

Danny's eyes opened before Simon's feet hit the top step on the stairs. He was sitting up and slipping his shoes on by the time he entered the room.

'Time to go,' was all Simon said before turning and leaving the room.

'Don't you ever sleep?' Danny said after him.

'Rarely, Mr Pearson, rarely,' came Simon's reply from the stairs.

As Danny descended the stairs, a strong smell of petrol burned his nostrils. He reached the bottom and turned into the kitchen, stopping at the sight of Tyson and Billy. They were sitting upright on the kitchen chairs, their hands tied behind them and tape over their mouths. Their heads were slumped forward and their chins were stuck to the sticky sea of crimson blood that covered their fronts and dripped into the puddle on the floor from their slit throats.

'Was that quite necessary?' Danny said to Simon, who looked at Tyson and Billy with emotional indifference.

'Quite necessary, dear boy. They saw my face, and officially I was never here. It would be pointless to arrest them. One of Delany's briefs would have them out within the hour, and then Delany would know you were coming for him, and we can't have that, can we? When they eventually find their bodies, they'll link them to Mr Delany and put it down to rival drug dealers, or punishment for double crossing their boss. Now, if you wouldn't mind,' Simon said, gesturing for Danny to follow him.

They both walked out of the house onto the drive past two black-suited agents standing by the back door. There was no sign of the special ops team from earlier, just two cars waiting on the road below with the first signs of the new day lighting up the estuary behind them. The driver of the front vehicle opened the doors for Danny and Simon as they approached. As the car moved smoothly forward, there was a large whoosh of light and heat as Delany's house turned into a flaming inferno, the outline of the other two agents visible, lit up by the flames as they walked down the drive towards the second car.

'Where are we going?' Danny said.

'Southend Airport. I've got a very nice little G5 waiting to fly you to Alicante.'

'You're not coming?'

'Good God, no. A charming little man by the name of Hugo Serrano will be waiting for you when you get there. He's one of mine. He'll drive you around and get you whatever you need.'

'Why don't you get him to kill Delany?' Danny said sarcastically.

'Mmm, Mr Serrano has many talents. Killing people is not one of them. He's a fixer, not a killer. You need a gun, knife or explosives, he'll get it. You need to know where Delany is. Mr Serrano will know someone who knows.'

Danny didn't bother answering Simon. He turned his head and looked out of the car window, lost in his thoughts. The English countryside whizzed by outside, its detail getting clearer by the minute as the sun rose above the horizon. An hour later, the car pulled up outside the small private jet centre terminal, sitting to one side of the main airport terminal. Simon walked into the building ahead of Danny, smiling at the suited woman that greeted him warmly.

'Good morning, my dear, this is our VIP guest, Mr Pearson. I trust you will take great care of him,' Simon said, gesturing towards Danny.

'Of course, we've been expecting you, Mr Pearson. My name is Pamela. If you'd like to come this way, we'll get you checked in and on your way,' she said, turning to lead him to a check-in desk.

'I haven't got my passport or any money or clothes,' Danny said quietly to Simon as they approached the desk.

Before Simon could answer, the man on the desk brought up an envelope with a passport on top from behind the desk.

'Your personal assistant dropped your passport, itinerary and carry-on bag off some time ago, Mr Pearson. Here's your boarding pass, and your bag is already on the plane. The flight crew is all ready and waiting for you. If you would like to follow Pamela, she will show you on board.'

'Er, thanks,' Danny said, turning to follow Pamela while Simon walked away towards the exit.

'Have a good business trip, Daniel,' he said over his shoulder without looking back.

Pamela led Danny out of the terminal and across the

tarmac to a glistening white G5 Gulfstream. Two hostesses, the pilot and co-pilot, greeted him as he entered the plane.

'Good morning, sir. If you would like to take a seat, we have a take-off slot in about fifteen minutes. Once we are in the air, Sandy and Rachael will attend to your every need.'

'Great,' Danny said, feeling awkward at the attention. He moved into the seating area with its eight soft cream leather seats and large couch, recognising his tatty old kit bag from home sitting propped up on one side of the couch. Grabbing it, Danny sank into one of the super comfortable leather seats and checked inside. His jeans, some tops, underwear and wash bag were all inside. He put the bag down and opened the itinerary envelope to find two one-thousand-Euro bundles of cash and a mobile phone with Hugo Serrano's name and phone number on a post-it note stuck to the front of it. Danny's face went taut as he ground his teeth. The passport, envelope and bag all re-enforced the feeling that he'd been played by Simon yet again.

'Can I get you anything, sir?' said the hostess with Sandy written on her badge.

'Yes, I'll have a large whisky on the rocks,' Danny said, the need for a stiff drink growing as he thought back over the night's events.

CHAPTER 54

Simon hung around in the car park just long enough to see the G5 Gulfstream take to the air.

'Back to Whitehall, please, Trevor,' he said to his driver.

'Very good, sir.'

As they headed along the A127 heading towards London, Simon tapped a number and put his phone to his ear.

'Simon.'

'Good morning, sir, I apologise for the early hour, but I just thought you would like to know our man is in the air.'

'Thank Christ for that. He'd bloody well better kill Delany this time. I don't need another screw up, Simon.'

'With all due respect, Minister, considering the short amount of time you gave us to orchestrate the last attempt to neutralise Delany, I'm amazed it went as well as it did. Getting my agent into Mr Delany's house as his girlfriend was hard enough, without acquiring the memory stick to lure him out of the country to Benidorm. And don't forget this all had to be done to coincide with Mr Pearson and his friends' visit. In fact, if Alonzo Acosta hadn't kidnapped Mr Miller and my two agents, the chances are they would have succeeded in manipulating Mr Pearson into killing Delany, instead of doing a deal with him for their safety.'

'Well, yes, I suppose so.'

'That being said, it's thanks to Mr Miller's involvement that we now have the leverage and motivation to make our man kill Mr Delany while maintaining full deniability of any agency involvement.'

'Yes, that was very fortuitous for us. You're sure Delany is heading to Spain?'

'Yes sir, Mr Pearson got the information from two of Delany's men, and we confirmed it when we questioned them ourselves. He's going to see Samuel Mendez before travelling to the Sudan. We don't know how he intends to get there, but my best guess is he'll take a boat to Algeria or Libya and fly - without fear of being detained - from there to the Sudan,' Simon said, without a thought of the fate of Tyson and Billy.

'Good, and what of your two female agents?'

'They have been redeployed overseas for the foreseeable future.'

'Very well. Just let me know when it's done. We need to seal this lithium deal before the Chinese or Americans get their hands on it.'

'Yes sir,' Simon said, hanging up.

He leaned back in his seat, closed his eyes and let out a long sigh.

'Are you all right, sir?' asked Trevor, his eyes on Simon in the rear view mirror.

'Fine, thank you, Trevor. It's been a long night, that's all.'

'We will need to make a quick stop for fuel, sir.'

'Better that than to have an electric car,' Simon muttered to himself.

'Sorry sir?'

'That's fine, Trevor.'

CHAPTER 55

'Where are we going?' Delany said, waking up with a start to see them driving past the signs for Benidorm.

'Mr Mendez thought it might be safer not to go to the club or his villa. We are to take you to a citrus farm a friend of his owns on the outskirts of Altea. We will be there shortly,' said Arlo.

'Is Mendez there?'

'No, Mr Mendez will join you later. He has to take care of some things first.'

Delany eyed Arlo's reflection in the rear view mirror with paranoid suspicion, his hand sliding inside the bag to rest on the Glock handgun hidden out of sight. He eventually relaxed his grip, accepting what Arlo said when he saw the relaxed indifference in Arlo's reflection in the rear view mirror. Fifteen minutes later, Arlo turned off the main road onto a long tree-lined gravel track. They rumbled along for another mile, listening to ticks and cracks as the tyres flicked up small stones into the underside of the wheel arches like tiny bullets fired from a gun.

The track eventually opened out into a larger gravel driveway, lit up by lights coming from a white rendered traditional hacienda style farmhouse. Delany's hand found the butt of his gun again as the front door opened, relaxing when he recognised a couple of Mendez's men. Arlo and Javier got out and greeted the men in Spanish as they approached the door. Delany got out a moment later, the Glock from his bag now transferred into the waistband of the back of his trousers, hidden from view under his jacket.

'Welcome, Mr Delany, please come in. We have food if you are hungry, or pick a bedroom if you are tired after your journey,' said Mendez's man.

'Where is Mendez?' Delany snapped back at him.

'Mr Mendez had to visit his business partners in Barcelona. He said it was to fetch the package you required for your visit to the Sudan. He will be back later today.'

Delany didn't move for a few seconds, then turned away from the guy without saying a word, carrying his bag up the stairs towards the bedrooms. Arlo and Javier watch him go. Arlo shrugged before heading towards the kitchen.

'Well, I'm going to eat. I'm bloody starving.'

Upstairs, Delany looked in a couple of rooms before picking a large bedroom with a big king-sized bed against the opposite wall, facing the door. He shut the door and dragged the chair by the dresser over to jam it under the handle so no one could enter. Placing the bag on one side of the bed, he drew the gun and laid it next to the bag. Exhausted and mentally drained, Delany lay down fully clothed and fell asleep, his right hand resting gently on the gun beside him.

CHAPTER 56

After a much needed two hour sleep on the plane, the air hostess woke Danny to tell him they would be landing shortly. He yawned and stretched, his joints aching and clicking after the stresses and strains of the last few days. The jet touched down onto the tarmac with the lightest of touches and taxied away from the main terminal used by the large aviation companies carrying hordes of package holidaymakers. It stopped outside the General Aviation Terminal dedicated to private jets. The engines wound down and the hostess opened the door to a waft of warm air even though it was early in the morning. Danny stepped out with his bag and thanked the crew as he exited. An overly smiley man in a grey suit greeted him at the bottom of the steps.

'Good morning, sir, I trust your flight was good,' he said, offering his hand to shake.

'Er, yeah, it was great, thanks,' Danny replied, shaking his hand quickly while continuing to walk towards the terminal.

'Excellent, my name is Milo. I'm the executive

customer relations manager,' the man said, quickening his steps to keep up with Danny. 'Sir, sir, I've been instructed to tell you that the jet will remain here at your disposal until midnight tonight. If you arrive after that time, you will have to make your own travel arrangements.'

Danny stopped in his tracks and turned, his face set as hard as stone with a look that could kill. 'Midnight,' he growled.

'Yes sir,' Milo said, Danny's look keeping him back beyond arm's reach.

'Midnight, fucking marvellous. I'm supposed to be getting married at eleven tomorrow morning,' Danny muttered, turning away to enter the terminal.

After a very informal security check, Danny exited the small terminal building onto the pavement next to the drop off bay. A couple dressed in designer clothes were getting into a luxury minivan in front of him. The chauffeur driver slid the side door shut and climbed into the driver's seat. He started it up and drove the vehicle smoothly away, opening up the view of the car park beyond. A short, scruffy, overweight man stood in centre view with his arms outstretched and a wide grin on his face.

'Hey, Mr Pearson, welcome to Spain, *hombre*, you want to go get some breakfast? A coffee? Something stronger?' Hugo shouted, opening the passenger door of an old Volvo for him.

'Just get in the damn car, Hugo,' Danny said grumpily, throwing his bag in the back as he got in and slammed the door shut.

'Ok man, so you're not a morning person, no problem. You can watch me eat,' Hugo said cheerfully, starting the car and grinding the gears into reverse to pull out of the parking place.

'Where's Delany?' Danny said, eager to get on with the job so he could get the hell out of there and back to the UK.

'I dunno,' Hugo said with a shrug, crunching the car in first and pulling out of the car park.

'What do you mean you don't know? It's your job to know.'

'I mean, I don't know. He's not at Club Desire or Mendez's villa. Mendez's main man, Arlo Hernandez, and Javier left the club yesterday in a hurry and haven't been seen since. As for Mendez himself, he is in Barcelona on business. Delany was still in England yesterday, so I'm guessing Arlo and Javier have gone somewhere to pick him up. Considering the distance from the UK to here he's probably not here yet. He may not even be in Spain yet. How do I know this? Because I was up half the night checking. Now, *señor*, I am hungry, I need some breakfast, ok?' said Hugo, turning onto the slip road to join the motorway to Benidorm.

Danny realised he was being a bit of a prick and pushed his bad mood aside. 'Coffee and a full English, none of that little plate tapas shit,' Danny said with a smile.

Hugo looked blankly across at Danny before his face broke into a grin. 'Coffee and a full English, no problem.'

'So what's your story, Hugo? You don't look like one of Simon's usual agents.'

'I was a police detective in the drug squad, twenty years on the force. I got too close to Samuel Mendez and Gregory Delany's cocaine smuggling organisation. They had Arlo Hernandez break into my house while we slept.

He killed my wife and six-year-old daughter. I got shot five times trying to stop him and he left me for dead.'

'Shit, I'm sorry, mate. How come he didn't go down for murder?'

'When I came out of a coma three months later and told them it was Hernandez, my colleagues arrested him, but later had to let him go. He had witnesses and fake CCTV footage putting him at Club Desire all night.'

'That was it? He just got away with it?' Danny said, shaking his head.

'Yes, that and the forensic evidence that magically went missing. Delany and Mendez have several officers on the payroll,' Hugo said with a melancholy tone in his voice.

'So what happened to you?'

'Because of my injuries they pensioned me off, and after several painful months of rehabilitation I left the hospital to an empty house and a full bottle of drink. After weeks in a drunken haze, I bought a gun and staggered over to Club Desire to kill Hernandez, to kill them all. Before I got there, two men grabbed me and threw me into the back of a car with a suited man.'

'Simon.'

'Yes, Simon, he said if I went into the club, they would kill me before I got ten feet. He was right, I was blind drunk. I probably would have shot myself before I hit one of them. He told me that if I helped him, using my local knowledge and contacts gained from my years in the police force, he would make sure they paid for what they did to my family. And here you are.'

'I'm only here to kill Delany,' Danny said bluntly.

'I have money, thirty thousand euros, kill Arlo Hernandez and it's yours.' Hugo said, the happy-go-lucky grin gone from his face.

Danny looked across at Hugo, but said nothing for a long time. His mind ticked over Hugo's story and offer.

'I'm not a mercenary, or a paid assassin, Hugo, I'm here because Delany has put a price on my head and the only way to remove it is to kill him so I can get on with my life,' Danny eventually said.

'At least you have a life to get on with. Hernandez ended my life when he took my wife and daughter,' Hugo said bluntly.

'I won't take your money. But I promise you, if Arlo Hernandez tries to stop me from killing Delany, I will kill him.'

'Thank you, my friend. I will have to settle for that.'

The drive fell into an awkward silence for a while.

'Simon said you can get me what I need for the job,' said Danny, finally breaking the tension in the car.

'In the glove box,' Hugo said, his grin returning.

Danny opened the glove box. An assortment of handguns and spare magazines rattled forward.

'Ok, I was hoping to pick him off from a distance with a rifle, an AR-15, M4 or M16 with Razor or EOTech sights,' Danny said, closing the glove box.

'Back seat,' Hugo said without taking his eyes off the road.

Danny turned himself sideways and looked at the thick patterned blanket on the back seat. He moved his rucksack to one side and lifted the blanket to see a desert camouflage AR-15 assault rifle, complete with Vortex Razor sights.

'You could have at least put it in the boot,' Danny said, lowering the blanket.

'Not a good idea, there's no room in the boot,' Hugo said with a grin.

'Why? What's in the boot?' Danny said, his curiosity piqued.

'Just something I had to pick up on the way to the airport. Don't worry, he's still sleeping. We will go for breakfast first,' said Hugo, turning off the motorway at the junction for Benidorm.

'Sleeping? What? Who's sleeping?'

'One of Mendez's guys, Mateo Guilar, I injected him with ketamine as he left his apartment. It'll be another hour before he's awake and in any state to question about where Delany is.'

Danny looked at the back seat as if he could see through it into the boot, then at Hugo. 'Now I see why Simon picked you.'

CHAPTER 57

Hugo took Danny to an English cafe-cum-bar on the outskirts of Benidorm, parking the old Volvo on the road outside so they could keep an eye on it from the outside table.

'Do you think he's alright in there?' Danny said, looking up to feel the heat from the rising morning sun.

'Maybe he is, maybe he's not,' Hugo said, shrugging with emotional indifference before waving to the waiter.

They ordered two large breakfasts and lots of coffee from the waiter, who turned out to be from Enfield in North London. The injection of food and the caffeine hit from several coffees pushed the fatigue from Danny's lack of sleep away, allowing clarity of thought to return. As the waiter placed the bill on the table, dull thuds and muffled screams emanated from Hugo's boot, causing all three of them to turn their heads towards the car. Danny grabbed the waiter's wrist in a vice-like grip, causing the man to look down in panic.

'This is for the food, and this is for you. You heard

nothing, ok?' Danny said, tucking a hundred and fifty euros into the waiter's top pocket while looking unwaveringly into the his eyes.

'Thanks, you have a good day, guys,' the man said, giving Danny a nod before turning and walking inside to mind his own business.

'Time to take our friend somewhere quiet for a chat,' Hugo said, seemingly unbothered by the noise coming from his boot.

They got up and went to the car. Hugo banged on the boot and shouted, 'Shut up in there,' as he walked around to the driver's side and got in.

They pulled off in a cloud of diesel smoke and headed back out of Benidorm.

'Where are we going?' Danny said.

'Just out of town, there's a development that ran out of money. Very quiet, nobody around,' Hugo replied.

Ten minutes later they drove up the rising hills before turning down a rough access road. The tarmac ran out, leaving the car rumbling loudly along a packed hardcore surface that ran between a row of concrete block skeletal shells of luxury villas, with panoramic views of Benidorm and the sea beyond.

'Pass me a gun,' Hugo said, pointing to the glove box.

Danny passed him one and took one for himself. They both got out of the car and walked around to the boot.

When they opened it, Mateo Guilar put his hands up in front of his face, blinking blindly against the sudden sunlight, confusion and fear written all over his face and a piss stain darkening his trousers.

'You motherfucker, you piss all over my car! I should shoot your sorry ass right here,' Hugo shouted in rapid

Spanish, jabbing his gun at Mateo to add to the intimidation.

As Mateo's eyes adjusted to the light, he looked from Hugo to Danny, his face switching from confusion to fear as recognition kicked in.

'Please, don't kill me, I'm nobody. I just run errands for Mendez,' Mateo pleaded in broken English.

Tucking the gun in the back of his trousers, Danny reached in and yanked Mateo clean out of the boot, dumping him painfully onto the rough, stony surface. Mateo groaned and rolled to one side, looking up just in time to see Danny's fist hurtling towards his face. Pain rattled around his head as Danny's knuckles made contact with his bruised, fractured cheekbone.

'You've got one chance and one chance only, tell me where Delany is or I kill you, right here, right now,' Danny growled, pulling the gun from his trousers and pulling the slide to chamber a round before he pushed the barrel up under Mateo's chin.

'Wait, wait, I don't know where he is, please.'

'Think of your mama, Mateo, how she's going to feel. He's going to shoot you in the face if you don't give us something. They'll have to bury you with a closed casket,' Hugo said, crouching down to talk quietly into Mateo's ear.

'I swear I don't know where he is.'

'Kill him, he's of no use to us,' said Hugo, standing up with seeming indifference to whether Mateo lived or died.

Danny played along and locked his arm out straight so that Mateo had to look along the barrel of the gun and plead with him not to pull the trigger.

'I don't know where Mendez is hiding him, but I know who does,' Mateo said, tears running down his cheeks as he cowered on the floor, expecting a bullet and lights out any second.

'Spit it out, and I'll know if you're lying,' Hugo said, reverting back to Spanish.

'Yesterday, before Mendez left for Barcelona, he had the chef prepare food for Delany's arrival. The chef had Esteban, the kitchenhand, deliver it. Esteban knows where they are taking Delany,' Mateo blurted out as quickly as he could.

'What's this kid look like, and where do we find him?' Hugo said, giving a small nod to Danny, who hadn't understood a word they'd said, to let him know they were making progress.

'He's a tall, skinny kid with dark hair to his shoulders. He'll be at the club by now, preparing food before the chef gets in,' Mateo said through the pain in his head, his eye blackening and already swelling shut.

'We've got to go to the club. The kitchenhand, a guy named Esteban, delivered food to wherever they are hiding Delany,' said Hugo, turning to Danny.

'What do we do with him?' Danny said, looking at Mateo's snivelling body.

'I don't know man, you wanna, you know, pow pow,' Hugo said, making the movement of shooting with his gun.

'No, I don't want pow bloody pow. I told you, I'm not a murderer. This idiot is no threat to me,' Danny said, annoyed.

'Ok, ok,' Hugo replied, tucking his gun into his waistband before feeling in his pocket to bring out a pair of handcuffs. 'Bring him into the shade and I'll cuff him to one of the reinforcing rods. No one comes up here. I'll come back and let him go when we're finished.'

They manhandled Mateo into one of the skeletal villas and handcuffed him up underneath the concrete stairs to the first floor. Returning to the car, Hugo got a bottle of water from the back and left it with Mateo before spinning the car around in a cloud of dust and headed back towards Benidorm.

CHAPTER 58

Gregory Delany's eyes shot open, his hand already gripping the gun beside him as his heart pounded. He sat up, the overload from the events of the last couple of days temporarily fogging his mind to make him question where the hell he was. Seconds later it all fast-forwarded like a time-lapsed camera feed to his arrival last night. Blinking the sleep away, he looked at his watch, surprised to see it was after midday. He got out of bed, the enormity of what he'd lost hitting home as he looked out of the hacienda window at the orange groves. Delany was never one to wallow in self pity, he planned to push Omar Al Nuran hard to supply him more cocaine, with the promise of more funding for his paramilitary group, the RSF. With Mendez and Ken working the dealer network to the limit while he was getting plastic surgery and a new identity in South Africa, Delany could return to the UK triumphant as the cocaine king with a new name and a new face. He freshened up in the ensuite bathroom then headed downstairs, still keeping hold of his bag and with his gun tucked in the back of his trousers. When he entered the kitchen Mendez and Arlo were sat at the table looking back at him.

'Good to see you safe and sound, Gregory,' Mendez said, getting up to shake Delany's hand.

'Did you get the money?' Delany said, ignoring the pleasantries.

'A million five,' Mendez said, turning his head and nodding towards two large canvas bags in the corner.

Delany smiled for the first time in days. 'Good, and Nazim's yacht to Béjaïa?'

'Nazim should arrive at Altea's marina any time now. I have men waiting to pick up our shipment of cocaine, and he will have to refuel before you leave. You should be good to go by around six.'

'Can I trust Nazim?' Delany said, his eyes looking at the one and a half million euros sitting in the canvas bags in the corner.

'Totally, he's been bringing in our shipments for the last two years, no problems, and I'm sending Arlo with you until you get on the plane to Béjaïa,' Mendez said, offended by Delany's lack of trust in him.

Delany looked at Arlo like he was dog shit he'd just stepped in. 'You, get me some coffee and food,' he said, just to push Arlo's buttons.

Arlo's eyes burned angrily at being ordered around like Delany's bitch, but he knew his place and walked over to the kettle without saying anything.

'We need to discuss what we do about the ice cream factory. Now that the authorities are suspicious, we need another packing plant,' said Delany, turning his attention back to Mendez.

'It is all in hand, but it's going to cost.'

'How much?' Delany said, frowning.

'The man I went to see in Barcelona has a factory we can use. He put up half the money over there for ten percent of the profit. My men are fitting out the factory as we speak, only difference is we will have to deliver the ice cream from here before repackaging.'

'Ten percent of your end,' Delany said, as more of a statement than a question.

'Of course,' Mendez answered calmly.

'Good. I left Ken in charge back home while I'm away, we're changing the safe houses and supply routes as a precaution. I want to double supply by the time I return.'

'How long do you think that will be?' Mendez said, leaning back as Arlo thumped a cup of coffee down on the table followed by a plate of meats and breads before walking out of the room.

'Two, maybe three months, as long as the plastic surgery takes to heal.'

Mendez nodded without comment, sitting back deep in thought as Delany ate and drank his coffee.

CHAPTER 59

'How are you going to get this Esteban out of there so we can question him?' Hugo said, the two of them sitting in the parked car looking at Club Desire. Even with the car windows down, both men sat sweating uncomfortably under the midday sun.

'Fucked if I know. This kid gets in before the chef, yeah?'

'That's what Mateo said.'

'Well, I haven't got time to fuck about. I'll just have to go and get him. The club isn't open to the public for a few hours, so hopefully there'll only be this Esteban and the odd member of bar staff or cleaner,' Danny said, more to convince himself than anything else.

'Excellent plan. I'll wait here, my friend. Good luck,' Hugo said with a grin.

Danny just looked at Hugo and sighed. 'Great, thanks,' Danny replied, pushing the door open and heading off around the back of the club.

The courtyard to the rear was empty apart from the van still parked in the same spot as before. The club's rear fire door was wedged open, presumably to let some air into the kitchen. Tired, irritated and impatient, Danny pulled the gun from the back of his jeans and walked straight through the door. The corridor was clear as he moved inside. Ignoring the stars dancing in front of his vision as his eyes adjusted from the harsh sunlight outside, Danny swung into the kitchen to see a skinny young man fitting the description of Esteban chopping vegetables with his back to him. Danny moved swiftly forward and placed the muzzle of the gun onto the back of Esteban's head.

'You speak English?' he asked.

'Yes, a little, please don't hurt me,' Esteban said, raising his hands to either side of him.

'No one's going to get hurt. I just need you to follow me outside so I can have a word with you, ok? Now, put the knife down and back up with me towards the door,' Danny said, keeping his voice calm.

'Yes, ok,' said Esteban, following Danny's instructions.

As he backed up to the doorway, Danny bumped into something solid. Before he could turn to see what it was, the chef's massive hand reached over him and grabbed his gun. The jolt from the chef ripping it from Danny's hand pulling on his trigger finger. The gun went off, sending a round through the flesh on the outside of Esteban's shoulder. Estaban screamed out in pain and staggered back into the kitchen.

Hundreds of training hours and muscle memory from his time in combat kicked in. Danny dropped and rammed his elbow back into the mountain of a man's bollocks, immediately shooting back upright while throwing his head back to crunch the back of his skull into the chef's face. Hearing the gun clatter to the floor, Danny jumped forward and turned, expecting to see the chef falling to the ground. Instead of looking down, he had to look up at the chef's face as it contorted angrily through the blood running from his nose. His tree trunk arms shot out and two dinner plate-sized hands grabbed Danny around the throat, lifting him clean off the floor. Unable to breathe and with his head feeling like it was about to pop, Danny fell back on his self defence training. He whipped his left arm up and over the top of the chef's wrists, powering the bony part of his elbow down to bend the chef's hands back until the pain made him release the grip on Danny's throat.

Dropping to his feet, Danny sucked great gulps of air into his lungs. Ignoring his spinning head, he launched a blistering combination of punches to the chef's kidneys before stepping forward and powering an elbow up into the chef's chin. The blow should have felled an elephant, but only managed to rock the chef. He stepped back and shook his head before charging at Danny with a snarl on his face. Danny retreated, only to be stopped when his back hit a stainless steel preparation table. He reached behind him and grabbed the first thing he came across. Whipping it forward, Danny powered it in and out of the chef's chest. His hand was a blur until it stopped with the last blow hammering up under the chef's chin. Danny let go and stood back, leaving only the handle of the six-inch chopping knife visible under the chef's chin. The giant of a man dropped heavily to his knees, his eyes dull and life-less as he fell forwards, slapping onto the kitchen floor. In the space where the chef had stood, Danny saw Esteban legging it out the door.

'Oh for fuck's sake,' Danny said, seeing his dropped gun and picking it up.

Jumping over the chef's dead body, Danny hurtled out

the door after the skinny young man. Sitting in the car outside, Hugo jumped upright in his seat at the sight of Esteban flying out from behind the club, running like a man possessed with a bloody shoulder and a look of terror on his face. A second later Danny powered out after him, his gun swinging in his blood covered hand.

'Hugo. Car,' he yelled as he powered down the road after Esteban.

Hugo started the car and drove forwards, screeching left before screeching left again. He floored the old Volvo, craning his neck to look down every side street until he caught sight of Danny giving chase on the road parallel to him.

Danny ran as fast as he could, his eyes zeroed in on his target thirty metres ahead of him. But Esteban was young, skinny and powered by fear and adrenaline. Trying as hard as he could, Danny couldn't close the gap between them. He twisted to get a quick look behind him, surprised not to see the old Volvo about to pass him.

Where the fuck is Hugo?

To make matters worse, they were running into a busier area. A group of lads let out a drunken cheer from a bar as Esteban flew past in the middle of the road. Danny quickly tucked the gun into his jeans and covered it with his shirt, the move slowing him down enough to lose another five metres on Esteban. Just when he thought he'd have to give up, the Volvo shot out of a side street, its bonnet dipping as Hugo stamped on the brakes and side-swiping Esteban's legs from under him, sending him bouncing off the bonnet onto the floor on the other side of the car. Hugo leaped out and grabbed Esteban as he rolled about groaning, dragging him into the back seat as Danny caught up.

'Where the. Fuck. Have you. Been?' Danny said in between breaths.

'What the hell happened in there?' Hugo replied, getting back into the driving seat.

'The bloody chef turned up,' Danny said, still out of breath as he jumped in the back, grabbing hold of Esteban with one hand while shoving the gun in his face with the other as Hugo drove off as fast as the Volvo would go.

'Don't kill me,' Esteban yelled, tears rolling down his eyes.

'Just shut the fuck up a minute,' Danny said, sweating profusely as he tried to compose himself. 'Ok, listen to me. Yesterday you took the food to a house for Mr Mendez. I need that address.'

'If I tell you, you'll kill me,' snivelled Esteban.

'Listen, you little shit, I'm hot, I'm sweaty, I'm out of breath, and I'm in a really fucking bad mood. Just tell me where the house is and I'll drop you off on the outskirts of town, ok? Don't tell me, and I'm going to start pulling the trigger until you do. *Comprende*?' Danny growled, moving the gun from Esteban's face to make him jump when he jabbed the muzzle into his groin.

'Ok, ok, I'll tell you,' Esteban blurted out in a panic.

CHAPTER 60

'Is that the yacht?' Delany asked for the fourth and every time that Mendez had answered his phone.

Mendez continued his stream of incomprehensibly fast Spanish while nodding in Delany's direction. Over the other side of the kitchen, Arlo got up off his chair and wandered over to Javier. He leaned in and whispered something into his ear and the both of them turned and left the room.

'We are all good. Nazim has unloaded the shipment to my men with no problem. He has sent some of his guys to get supplies for the journey back and is refuelling the yacht. He will call when they are ready to leave. It shouldn't be long.'

'Good, I can't wait to get going,' Delany said, silenced by Mendez's phone ringing.

'Sorry, I've got to get this. It's the club,' Mendez said, cutting Delany short to answer it.

As Delany waited impatiently, Mendez's face fell. The look immediately vanished to be replaced by a deep frown.

'What is it? What's wrong?' Delany demanded.

'The chef is dead. Somebody shoved a kitchen knife into his brain.'

'Who did it?' said Delany, automatically looking out the windows as if he were being watched.

'They don't know. There are no cameras in the kitchen and the kitchen hand, Esteban, is missing.'

'What, did this Esteban kill him?'

'I don't think so. They tell me that Mateo hasn't turned up for work either and nobody can get hold of him. I think we should get you to the yacht. You'll be safe there until it sails and I can find out what the hell is going on.'

'Ok, get that useless lump, Arlo, to put the money into the car. I'll get my bag,' Delany said.

'Arlo,' Mendez shouted towards the door, as Delany picked his bag up from one of the kitchen chairs.

When Arlo didn't come, Mendez shouted again, a look of frustration on his face when he still didn't show. 'He must be outside.'

'Fucking unless lump,' Delany said angrily.

Both men walked through the kitchen door into the main hall, with its grand staircase leading to the bedrooms beside them and the front door ahead. Arlo and Javier stood on either side of the front door, two of Mendez's men lying dead at their feet. Arlo had slit the throat of one, the arterial spray painting zig zags across the white plastered wall behind him. Javier had stabbed the man by his feet several times. He lay on the floor groaning while desperately trying to stem the flow of blood seeping out through his fingers.

'What the fuck are you doing?' Mendez yelled in Spanish.

'There has been a change of plan,' Arlo replied as he

and Javier raised their guns in Delany and Mendez's direction.

CHAPTER 61

'Do you see anything?' Hugo asked, laying on his front next to Danny.

'No, I can't see anyone,' Danny said, looking along the rows of orange trees towards the rear of the hacienda through the Vortex sight on the AR-15 rifle.

'Where are they all?' Hugo muttered.

'Stay here, I'm going for a closer look,' Danny said, getting up. He moved the gun from the back of his jeans to the front for faster access and headed off down the line of orange trees with the rifle up, its barrel moving as one with his line of sight.

'How will I know if you are ok?' Huge called after him.

'Just stay here. I'll call you on your mobile,' Danny answered without looking back.

Hugo watched him all the way to the end of the tree line. He went down on one knee while searching the rear windows of the hacienda for movement through the rifle sights. Seconds later he was up, running at full pelt through the grass before leaping up onto the terrace. He crossed to the back of the hacienda, flattening himself against the wall beside the doors to the kitchen. Sweat trickled down Hugo's face as he watched Danny duck his head across to look inside. A second later he gently opened the door and slid inside, then nothing. Hugo waited for the shouts and gunfire, but none came, his stare and concentration so intense that he jumped out of his skin when his mobile rang.

'*Si*.'

'You'd better come and see this,' Danny said, hanging up without saying more.

Hugo walked to the hacienda, tentatively poking his head inside the terrace doors to look inside the empty kitchen.

'Danny?' he shouted, taking a step inside.

'Through here, in the hall.'

Hugo followed Danny's voice to see him standing between two bodies lying by the front door. 'Did you kill them?'

'What? Oh, no. Look,' Danny said, nodding towards the staircase.

Turning around, Hugo saw the bodies of Gregory Delany and Samuel Mendez lying on the lower steps. Delany had a surprised look on his face and a bullet hole in the middle of his forehead. Mendez lay beside him with several bullet holes through his blood-soaked shirt.

'Jesus. Arlo! Is Arlo here?'

'No,' Danny said, spinning around at the sound of groaning coming from the man on the floor.

Squatting down, Danny turned him over. The man opened his eyes and grabbed Danny's forearm. He said something in Spanish, blood bubbling from his mouth as he spoke, until he fell silent and closed his eyes.

'What did he say?' Danny said to Hugo.

'He says Arlo double crossed them and took the money.' Hugo leaned in close. 'Where did he go?'

When he didn't answer, Hugo slapped the guy's face, forcing him to open his eyes again.

'Where did Arlo go?' Hugo shouted at him.

'Altea's marina, Nazim's yacht, The Ocean Blue. Arlo, he's heading to the Sudan to take over the entire operation,' the man's face contorted with pain. He arched his back and gasped his last breath.

Unable to understand Hugo and the man speaking Spanish, Danny wandered over and checked Delany's pulse, just to make sure he was dead. With his target taken care of, Danny checked his watch and mentally started planning his journey back to the jet, getting home, getting some shuteye before getting married.

'Arlo is sailing to Africa to take over the entire network. We've got to stop him,' Hugo said, walking up beside Danny.

'Sorry, Hugo, it's not my fight, this is me done, mate. Delany's dead and I'm free to get on with my life,' Danny said, looking down to see Hugo's face drop.

'Arlo is an evil man, worse than Delany or Mendez ever were. If he takes control, many more will die by his hand, and many, many more from his drugs. I don't want anyone else to go through what I went through. You are getting married, yes? Maybe one day you will have kids. I hope you never have to watch your wife and child die.'

'Hugo.' Before he could say any more, the memories and emotions from the deaths of his first wife and child, slaughtered by the psychopath Nicholas Snipe, choked him up and all he could do was stand and stare at Hugo.

'Fine, give me the rifle and gun then. Maybe it's finally time for me to stand up and kill the man who ruined my life,' Hugo said, a steely determination coming over him as he took the rifle from Danny.

Danny stood, conflicted, looking at the short round man clumsily holding the rifle with no idea what he was doing.

For fuck's sake, he's going to get himself killed before he gets anywhere near Arlo.

Danny looked at his watch again, then back at Hugo accidentally releasing the magazine onto the floor.

Just leave, go home, get married. Fuck Hugo, I don't owe him anything.

But he couldn't. His empathy for the man losing his family and his hatred for men like Arlo forced him to go with the only option he could live with.

'Give me that here before you blow your bollocks off,' Danny eventually said with a grin. 'Well don't just stand there. Bring the car around so you can take me to this bloody yacht.'

Hugo's face lit up. He slapped Danny on the back before heading out the front door of the hacienda.

'And hurry, I've got to be on that plane before midnight,' Danny called after him. He watched Hugo run to get the car from the farm track on the other side of the orange trees.

What the hell are you doing, you fucking idiot? This is a really bad idea.

CHAPTER 62

'Arlo, my friend, it all went well, yes?' said Nazim from the sun deck at the top of his 100-foot luxury yacht.

'Just like I said it would. Are we ready to leave?' replied Arlo, grinning as he held up the bag of money while walking up the gangplank, Javier following behind him with the other bag of money.

'Soon, I'm just waiting for my men to return with the supplies for the trip. They won't be long. Come, let's toast a new era. I have a bottle of champagne on ice inside.'

'I've just got to make a call first. Here, take the money down with you. I will be there in a minute,' Arlo said, handing his bag to Nazim before turning to Javier. 'Keep your eyes on the money,' he whispered. Javier nodded before following Nazim inside.

As soon as they were out of sight, Arlo made his call.

'Is it done?' came Kenneth Gambit's voice.

'Yes Ken, Delany and Mendez are dead. We now run the largest drug smuggling network in Europe.'

'Excellent, and your meeting with Omar Al Nuran is all set up?' said Ken.

'All set up. He said he is looking forward to doing business with us and thanked us for our generous donation to the RSF.'

'I'm glad he likes it. That was every penny I had,' Ken grumbled.

'Don't worry my friend, that will soon feel like small change.'

'Let's hope so. Be safe. Call me after the meeting,' replied Ken, ending the call.

Arlo stood on deck, holding his hand up to shield his eyes against the dipping sun. He looked slowly around the marina. Apart from some guys launching their jet skis from the beach just outside the marina, nothing stood out to alarm him. With a smile on his face, he turned and went inside the main deck. The yacht oozed the wealth and luxury that Arlo had been planning for himself for a very long time. Nazim and Javier sat on the soft white leather sofas in the lounge area while one of Nazim's men came out of the kitchen to serve chilled champagne.

'Not bad, eh? Let us go up to the bridge deck while we wait for my men to return,' Nazim grinned, raising a glass to Arlo.

'Not bad at all, I might have to get one of these for myself,' Arlo grinned back, taking a glass off the server.

'Here's to a very profitable partnership,' Nazim said, raising his glass to the others.

CHAPTER 63

'So what do we do when we find them?' Hugo said, his nerves showing in his voice.

'You just stick to my back like glue. Anyone comes at you while I'm dealing with what's in front and you shoot first, ask questions later. Can you do that, Hugo?' Danny said, his voice low and calm as he stopped checking the two handguns to look at Hugo and wait for his answer.

'Yes, I can do that. I will do that,' said Hugo, taking his eyes off the road for a second to look back at Danny.

'Good man. Now, where's this marina?'

'It is just at the end of the beach. See, up there, you can see the top of the masts,' Hugo said, pointing up ahead as he turned onto the seafront with La Roda beach on their left.

Danny looked ahead to see the masts. The view of the marina itself was still hidden from view by a harbour wall curling out in front of the marina, protecting it from rough seas. The two jet skiers enjoying some early evening fun before the sun went down, ripped up and down close to the wall. Danny and Hugo drove past them and parked the car opposite the rows of different types and sizes of yachts moored up to long walkways jutting out into the marina.

'Shit, what was the name of the yacht?' Danny said, stepping out of the car and looking out at the marina.

'The Ocean Blue,' Hugo said, stepping out of the other side of the car.

'The Ocean Blue, The Ocean Blue,' Danny muttered repeatedly, his eyes scanning up and down the rows of boats.

'You see it?'

'No,' Danny said, pausing as he looked out to where the marina opened out to sea, a frown suddenly etching its way across his forehead. 'Wait, er, fuck, fuck.' Danny's head whipped to the side as he looked to the beach on the other side of the harbour wall.

'Huh?' Hugo said, puzzled.

'Get a boat,' Danny said, taking off at a full sprint.

'Get a what?'

'Get a fucking boat and follow that. The bloody Ocean bloody Blue,' Danny shouted between breaths, his arm stabbing air as he pointed to The Ocean Blue yacht moving out of the marina.

'Oh, right, shit, get a boat, yes, er, get a boat. But where the hell is he going?' Hugo said, his eyes following Danny's pointing until he saw The Ocean Blue leaving the marina which made him jump into action, his head swinging this way and that before he ran towards the moored-up boats.

Danny sprinted across the road that ran along the harbour breakwater. He leapt up onto a low concrete wall on the far side and kept running along its top while looking past the piled up granite rock sea defences to the calm blue Mediterranean Sea. Seeing his target, Danny leaped off of the wall, bouncing from foot to foot as he hurtled his way precariously down the giant granite rocks before diving at the jet skier as he headed back towards the beach. With his arms wide, Danny hit the guy in a hard shoulder tackle, knocking him clean off the jet ski. As he thrashed around in the water, shocked, winded and in pain, Danny dragged himself onto the jet ski and opened it up. The front of the ski lifted out of the water as he gained speed, following the outside of the harbour wall towards the mouth of the marina, his eyes locking on to the top of The Ocean Blue's three decks just visible over the wall as it headed out of the marina on the other side.

Leaning over, Danny cornered around the end of the harbour wall, bouncing violently over the wake of the yacht as he cut across its stern. When the jet ski jumped out of the water off a wave, Danny used the upward momentum to leap onto the swim-up platform at the back of the yacht. Rolling as he landed, Danny flattened himself against the shiny white fibreglass hull, hidden from view by a small, solid hulled dinghy dangling from a swing out hoist above his head. Seeing a set of steps leading up past the dingy on either side of him, Danny reached for his gun, cursing when he realised he'd lost it knocking the man off his jet ski. He cursed again when he heard the engines wind up and saw the churning wash become more turbulent as the yacht increased its speed.

Feeling a sense of urgency, Danny moved up the steps until he could see across the main deck above. The outside space under the cover of the bridge deck, with a large dining table and bar, was empty, as was the lounge space visible inside through the open glass doors. Danny hopped up onto the deck and headed for the lounge. As he did, feet appeared, coming down a small spiral staircase to his right from the bridge deck above. With no time to hide and the man's jeans to his waist now visible, Danny grabbed the back of his trainers and pulled his feet from under him, sending him bouncing painfully into sight down the stairs. Nazim's Algerian deckhand's eyes went wide at the sight of Danny and his mouth opened to shout a warning. Danny powered punches into his face until the man's eyes rolled back in his head and he lay unconscious. Grabbing him by the feet, Danny quickly dragged him out of sight behind the bar on the open deck.

Heading inside to the plush lounge area, there were signs people had been there. Empty champagne glasses sat on the table with the empty champagne bottle sitting in the bucket full of melted ice beside them. Looking past the large dining table ahead of him, Danny weighed up whether to go through the door to what he guessed was the kitchen, or take the corridor to the side, leading to a small spiral staircase that went up to the bridge deck and down to the bedrooms on the lower deck. The decision was made for him when one of Nazim's men walked out of the kitchen munching on a sandwich. He froze mid-bite as the two men locked eyes.

Everything ran in slow motion. The man dropped his sandwich and went for his gun tucked in a shoulder holster. Danny started running, grabbing the neck of the empty champagne bottle on his way. Raising his arm to launch it, he jumped up and slid across the dining table toward Nazim's man. The bottle struck the guy in the forehead with its bottom edge, jerking the guy's head back as he pulled the trigger. The room filled with the deafening gunshot, Danny's feet hit the deck on the other side of the table. He kept moving forward and planted a powerful kick into the man's stomach, sending the gun flying as the man feet left the ground, sending him crashed backwards through the double hinged door into the large galley kitchen beyond.

CHAPTER 64

'What was that?' Arlo said, sitting up on the soft leather seats in the lounge area behind the bridge controls.

'It sounded like a gunshot,' Nazim said, getting up to open a cupboard and grab an AK-47 assault rifle, handing it to Arlo before fetching another one for himself.

'Stay here, and don't take your eyes off the money,' Arlo said to Javier.

'Akeem, keep the boat on course,' Nazim said to his man at the bridge controls before turning to look down the small spiral staircase to the main deck below.

'Did you see anyone near the boat while it was in the marina?' Arlo questioned Nazim.

'No, no one.'

'Go down and take a look,' Arlo gestured to Nazim.

'You go down and take a look,' Nazim replied, stepping back from the staircase.

'It's your fucking boat. Get your arse down the stairs,' Arlo growled back angrily.

'Ok, ok, fuck,' Nazim said, taking a tentative step

down the stairs with his rifle pointing out in front of him. He descended with his head low, so he could see into the lounge area as soon as possible. Relieved to see it empty, Nazim continued down the stairs, stepping onto the main deck, with Arlo following cautiously behind him.

'There's nobody here,' Arlo said, standing by the large dining table, looking through the open doors to the seating and bar area outside.

'Look,' Nazim said, running a finger along the scratched surface of the table with the empty champagne bottle lying on the floor by the kitchen door.

A groan from outside made them spin around in surprise. They moved cautiously through the lounge, stopping at the open glass doors with their AK-47s pointed ahead of them. A shaky hand appeared above the bar, gripping onto the top so he could haul himself upright. When the swollen face and broken nose of the deckhand came into view, Arlo and Nazim lowered their rifles. While Nazim questioned him over what had happened, Arlo headed back into the lounge, stopping by the kitchen door to lean his ear against the wooden surface. He could hear a buzzing sound from within.

'It's no good. He doesn't know who attacked him. All he remembers is being punched in the face,' said Nazim, moving over to Arlo with his sorry looking deckhand behind him.

'Shh, do you hear that?' Arlo said.

Nazim leaned in beside him and listened.

'What is that? You. Go in and find out,' Nazim ordered the deckhand, passing him the AK-47 before pushing the bruised, nervous man in front of him.

He pushed the door open slowly, sliding his head in

through the gap to see inside. As soon as he saw the room was empty, he relaxed and entered the kitchen.

'It's ok, no one is here,' he said to Nazim in Algerian.

Nazim nodded to Arlo and followed his man into the kitchen.

'The buzzing, it's just the microwave,' the deckhand said, approaching the machine as Arlo entered the room.

His eyes drawn to the lit-up window on the microwave, Arlo saw a can sparking to the microwave's casing as it turned in circles on the glass plate next to a couple of bags.

'Get out!' Arlo shouted, jumping back out of the swinging kitchen door.

As Nazim turned, the compressed can of lighter gas exploded, blowing the door into razor sharp pieces that embedded themselves into the deckhand's face. The explosion disintegrated the flour and sugar bags next to it, causing a huge cloud that engulfed the screaming deckhand, Nazim and the kitchen before the aerated powder ignited, turning the kitchen into a fiery inferno. Rolling away from the door on the lounge floor, Arlo covered his face as the kitchen door blew open, pushed by a massive ball of flame before swinging shut on the screams of Nazim and his deckhand still inside. By the time he'd got to his feet, the screaming had stopped and black smoke rolled around the edges of the kitchen door. Arlo picked up the AK-47 and moved out of the open glass doors to the outside seating area. He took a minute to get some air into his lungs, then headed up the spiral stairs to the bridge deck and Javier, and the money.

CHAPTER 65

After dumping Nazim's unconscious man in a guest bedroom on the lower deck, Danny took the man's gun and kitchen knife from his waistband and moved towards the rear of the boat. He stopped in his tracks and looked back when he heard and felt the microwave explosion go off on the deck above. When no one came rushing down the stairs after him, he continued into a small corridor with a heavy metal door in its centre. Looking through the small glass window, Danny spun the watertight locking wheel in the centre of the door and pulled it open, the noise from two large diesel engines hitting him as he stepped inside.

With a razor-sharp knife from the kitchen in one hand and the gun in the other, Danny had intended to cut the fuel lines to kill the engines and stop the boat. But when faced with the complicated array of wires and pipes on the two modern engines, he dropped the knife, tucked the gun in his waistband, and grabbed the fire extinguisher off the wall. Aiming at a box with a sizeable wiring loom disappearing into it, Danny rammed the end of the extinguisher into it over and over until the top eventually came off it. With one final smash the connections underneath sparked and smoked and the engine spluttered and died. An LCD control panel on the far wall started beeping and flashing with several red system errors.

Danny repeated the action on the second engine until that one died as well. He tossed the fire extinguisher and made his way towards the engine room door to a cacophony of beeping control panels. He opened the heavy watertight door to find the corridor filling with black acrid smoke. Danny quickly pulled the door closed again and took several deep breaths of clean air before heading back out. Holding his breath, and barely able to see where he was going, Danny made his way back through the bedrooms toward the small spiral staircase leading to the main deck above. When he got there he found that his improvised explosive device in the kitchen microwave had worked too well. Flames, black smoke and melting plastic whirled and dripped down the steps from above.

Left with the choice of going back towards the engine room of forward, Danny chose forward. With his lungs burning and eyes stinging in the thick smoke, he felt his way along the corridor until he came across a door at the front of the boat. He tried the handle to find it locked. Fighting the rising panic and spinning head, Danny stepped back and powered a kick into the door, breaking the lock. Stumbling into a storeroom, Danny took in the cylinders, diving equipment and metal steps leading to a hatch in the ceiling that opened out onto the open deck at the front of the yacht. The image vanished in a few seconds, swallowed up by the rush of thick black smoke flooding in through the open door.

Danny dived to the floor, taking a few deep breaths of clean air before the smoke filled the room. He shot his hands out and grabbed a diving cylinder and regulator. Being a seasoned diver, Danny easily attached the regulator to the cylinder without having to look at it. He sucked on the mouthpiece, relieved to breathe clean air, the luminous air pressure gauge showing just under 20bar. Not much, maybe three or four minutes of air. Danny climbed up the steps and started spinning the hatch locks. Feeling the air run out as he spun the last one, he cast the cylinder and regulator aside, pushed the hatch open and rolled out onto the deck at the front of the ship, sucking in great gulps of air as he looked up at the starry night sky, smoke rising from the hatch beside him.

With the dizziness in his head clearing, Danny wiped the water from his streaming eyes and stood up on the deck. The windows of the yacht were all black privacy glass, so he couldn't tell if anyone was inside. He pulled the gun out and looked up at the sundeck at the top of the boat. No one was up there. Danny looked down the narrow walkway leading to the back of the ship on the port side. Flames and smoke curled out of the blown-out kitchen window, making it impassable. He moved to the starboard side and headed to the rear of the yacht, thankful to see the walkway free of flames, and men with guns.

CHAPTER 66

'What was the explosion? The engines are dead, and where is Nazim?' said Nazim's man as Arlo came back onto the bridge deck.

Without warning, Arlo pulled the trigger on his AK-47, blowing the man into the cream leather seat where he flopped to one side, leaving a thick crimson smear on the upholstery.

'Grab a bag, we'll take the dinghy and get the fuck out of here,' Arlo said to Javier, while hooking the strap of the other money bag over his shoulder so it hung heavily on his back.

Javier didn't argue, he just grabbed the other bag and followed Arlo down the spiral staircase at the rear of the boat. Javier threw his bag into the dinghy while Arlo stabbed at the button to swing the hoist out over the swim-up platform.

'Come on, piece of shit,' Arlo shouted, punching the controls in frustration.

'Here, I'll do it,' said Javier, taking over the controls to lock the hoist out over the swim-up platform before lowering the dinghy into the sea.

As the bottom of the dinghy touched the water, Arlo turned around to climb down the steps to the swim-up platform and board the dinghy. As he looked ahead at the fire raging in the centre of the main deck, he saw Danny lit up by the flames as he moved outside the black privacy glass windows, heading towards him along the starboard side walkway.

'Fucking Pearson,' he growled, raising his AK-47 and pulling the trigger.

Javier ducked as rounds ripped through the boat, exploding the privacy glass windows into millions of crystal pieces as he moved in an arc towards Danny on the other side. Danny hit the deck, keeping his head down as glass rained down on him. As soon as Arlo's rifle clicked empty, Danny popped up onto his feet and ran towards the back of the boat, diving and shooting at Arlo across the outside seating area. In the same moment, Javier stood up, blocking Danny's view of Arlo and catching the three shots intended for him in his chest. As Javier fell to the floor, Arlo was already heading down the steps to the swim-up platform.

Danny picked himself up and ran after him, only getting a few feet when the propane cylinder in the kitchen exploded under the intense heat of the fire. The explosion ripped the centre of the boat apart, tearing its way up through the bridge and sundecks, and down through the lower deck and hull of the boat. The shockwave knocked Danny off his feet, his gun sliding across the deck and over the side, leaving his ears ringing and mind shocked into confusion.

When he dragged himself up onto his feet, Danny

thought his balance was shot, only to realise the yacht was listing heavily to one side. Gripping the handrail by the steps to the swim-up platform, he looked down to see Arlo unhook the dinghy from the hoist and start the little outboard engine. As the dinghy started moving away from the sinking yacht, Danny hopped over the railing, landing heavily on the swim-up platform. He pushed himself off the back wall in an explosion of power, taking the three steps like a long jumper before diving off the edge onto Arlo's back.

Both men tumbled painfully over the seat boards into the bottom of the little boat. Arlo rolled to one side, driving an elbow into Danny's chest, knocking him back against the outboard motor. The motor swung to one side, sending the boat turning in wide circles. Heaving himself upright with the money bag still on his back, Arlo grabbed the anchor chain at his feet and pushed the spring clip to detach the shackle from the ring at the front of the boat. As Danny sat upright, Arlo picked up the dinghy's double-spiked anchor and swung it around over his head by its chain, his eyes locked on Danny with murderous intent.

Danny stood, his legs slightly bent and hips loose, absorbing the movement of the little dinghy to keep his top half still while his eyes followed the movement of the anchor as it spun faster. He knew when Arlo was going to throw it, his body twisted to let his shoulder move back, ready for him to transfer power through his arm to launch the anchor forward.

Watching it come towards him in slow motion, Danny twisted sideways and leaned back. Already full of speed and momentum, the anchor whistled through the air towards his head. A flash of metal whizzed past Danny's eyes. He shot his hand up to catch the chain as it snapped tight by the anchor travelling as far as it could go. Yanking the chain towards him, Danny pulled Arlo off balance, helped by the rocking of the dinghy. Arlo went down on one knee, putting his hand down on its inflatable side to steady himself. Danny leaped at Arlo, the shift in weight making the dinghy lurch to one side, sending both men over the side into the sea.

Kicking with all his might to stay afloat against the waterlogged money bag still strapped to his back, Arlo gripped hold of Danny's top in one hand and spun the anchor chain tightly around his neck with the other. As Danny fought back, the anchor sunk to the length of the chain, instantly jerking Danny's neck back, dragging him under with barely time for a breath.

Sinking down past Arlo, Danny grabbed the money bag strap across Arlo's chest and yanked him under the surface with him. Danny's ears popped and the water temperature grew colder as they sunk deeper. Arlo thrashed around, trying to shake loose, while Danny clawed at the chain with his free hand to loosen it from his neck. He finally broke the friction holding chain against chain and it slipped off his neck to disappear into the murky depths. Both men stopped sinking, the money bag on Arlo's back stopping them from floating to the surface as they gripped each other tightly, their lungs bursting for air.

A burning rage flowed through Danny's body. Rage at Delany, who started all this, rage at Simon for manipulating him to come back, and rage at Arlo, the killer of Hugo's wife and child. Releasing the strap, Danny grabbed Arlo around the back of the head with both hands, pulling himself in as hard as he could to drive his forehead into Arlo's nose with a crunch. As he pulled his head back, he curled his thumbs around and pushed them into Arlo's eye sockets, digging them in until his eyeballs popped behind a silent scream of bubbles from Arlo's mouth.

Danny released Arlo. He jerked and convulsed before the weight of the money bag dragged him down into the dark water. With his head was spinning, Danny kicked for the surface, trying to suppress the building panic as his lungs burned. The surface never seemed to get any closer and with no sunlight above, he had no way of knowing how much further he had to go. With every ounce of oxygen burned up, Danny convulsed and blacked out to float motionless in the water.

CHAPTER 67

When he opened his eyes, nothing made sense. A face was staring down at him, the mouth forming a big grin, lit up by a flickering orange glow against the night sky.

'Welcome back. I thought for a minute you were dead,' said Hugo, helping Danny upright in the small wooden fishing boat.

Looking to his right, he saw the remains of the yacht burning brightly, its bow now submerged as the stern bobbed about, fully ablaze.

'We must go, there are boats coming because of the fire,' Hugo continued, turning back to wind up the outboard motor.

As Danny's head cleared, Hugo turned the fishing boat out to sea before taking a wide arc in the dark so they could slip past the half a dozen boats coming out of Altea marina to offer their assistance to the sinking yacht. While heading back, Danny spotted the empty dinghy from the yacht chugging its way to nowhere a little way ahead of them.

'Hugo, come alongside the dinghy,' Danny said, his throat sore from having the chain around it.

'*Si señor.*'

As they came side by side, Danny reached over the side of the fishing boat and grabbed the strap of the other money bag, yanking it up and into the boat.

'Ok, carry on, go, go.'

'What is that?' Hugo said, looking at the bag.

Danny unzipped it and showed him the bundles of money inside.

'Holy Mary Mother of God, what are you going to do with it?'

'Not me, Hugo. You do whatever you want with it, my friend. Keep it, give it away. Make a better life for yourself or someone else. Anything you like. Just promise me you won't work for the likes of Simon ever again,' Danny said.

'I have already decided I will not work for this man. You know he set you up, yes?'

'What? To make me come, yes, I know.'

'No, no, the first time. The two sisters, Sandra and Louise Benning, they are not sisters. That's not even their real names. They are two of Simon's agents. Running into you and staying at the same hotel, it was all a setup to make you kill Delany.'

'That fucking bastard did it again. Thanks for telling me, Hugo.'

'It's ok, I thought you should know. As for the money, I won't take the money for myself. There is an orphanage I know that is in danger of shutting down. This will ensure they remain open for many years.'

Danny nodded to him before looking at his watch and frowning. 'Shit! Hugo, I don't care how you do it, but make this thing go faster. I've got to get to Alicante airport before midnight.'

CHAPTER 68

'A ny news?' said Fergus, hurrying up the path to the church with Chaz and Danny's brother Rob standing outside.

'Any news about what?' said Rob, blissfully unaware of the events of the last few days.

'Er, well, we're not exactly sure where your brother is,' stammered Fergus, noting Chaz's shaking head to indicate he'd heard nothing from Danny.

'What do you mean not exact—'

'Hang on, Rob, Scott's calling,' said Fergus, cutting Rob short to answer the phone. 'Any news?'

'I'm afraid not. I was about to ask you the same question,' said Scott in a hushed voice so Nikki didn't hear him.

'No, I've called him and been round the house, there's no sign of him, and his phone just goes to voicemail,' said Fergus, feeling worse at hearing Nikki tell Scott that the wedding car was there and it was time to go.

'Sorry, chaps, I can't hold her back any more. We'll be

there in fifteen minutes. If he's not there, I'll just have to tell her,' said Scott, hanging up.

'No Scott. Shit,' Fergus said, tuning slowly to Chaz and Rob. 'She's on her way. What do we do?'

'I could fetch my sniper rifle and take out the driver. That'd slow them up,' said Chaz with a grin.

'That's not helping, Chaz,' said Fergus, the comment still making him chuckle.

'You two are like a couple of kids,' said Rob, frowning.

'Sorry, Rob. You go in, mate, and don't say anything to anyone, not just yet anyway.'

As Rob went inside, Fergus and Chaz stood worrying and checking their watches every thirty seconds.

'Do you think he's alright?' said Fergus.

'Yeah, bound to be. He's fucking indestructible, isn't he? He'll be here in a moment,' replied Chaz, trying to convince himself.

The minutes ticked by incredibly slowly. Chaz and Fergus walked to the end of the path to look up the long, straight road for the imminent arrival of the wedding car.

'Oh shit, there it is,' said Chaz, raising his voice over the rumble of a car and screeching tyres somewhere behind them.

'Someone should tell that wanker to drive more carefully. Doesn't he know there's a wedding on?' said Fergus, annoyed at the racket, both of them never taking their eyes off the approaching wedding car.

'Is that the bride?' came a voice from behind them.

'Yes, mate, but the groom's a no show,' said Chaz without looking back.

'So are you going to tell her or am I?' said Fergus to Chaz.

'Fuck that, mate, you're the best man, you tell her,' replied Chaz.

'Tell her what?' came the voice from behind.

'Listen, pal, do you mind? We're in the middle of having a fucking meltdown here,' Fergus said, turning to see Danny grinning back at them while straightening his tie and lifting his shirt collar a touch to cover the red chain marks on his throat.

'Tosser, where the hell have you been?' said Chaz, giving Danny a hug and a slap on the back.

'Come on, let's get inside before she sees us, I'll tell you about it later. Oh, and don't get your hopes up on seeing that Sandra Benning or her sister again, Chaz. They were both agents working for that bastard Simon,' Danny said, heading into the church.

'What, agents? Fucking hell, I really liked her as well.'

Danny greeted his small but select wedding guests, with his brother Rob and his wife Tina, niece Sophie and newborn niece Evie, his uncle Harry Knight and cousin May, and old friends Paul Greenwood, Thomas Trent, Big Dave Pullman and some of the lads from the gym, and Fergus's wife sitting next to Smudge's sister, Kelly. As Nikki had been in Australia for some years, and with her and Scott having no parents alive the same as Danny, her side only had a few of her old school friends and a couple of aunts and uncles. Danny made his way to the front with his best man, Fergus, by his side. He greeted the vicar and waited for Nikki to walk in with Scott, who was giving her away.

'You've got the rings, mate,' Danny said.

'Yeah, right here,' Fergus said, patting his pocket with a smile that fell as he patted it again.

'Fergus?'

'Right here, mate,' he replied with a big, cheesy grin.

'You toss—'

The organ drowned Danny's response out, piping up with the wedding march as the church door opened and Scott and Nikki walked in. Danny turned around and grinned at Nikki as she walked towards him, looking beautiful in her wedding dress. She stopped at the altar and they both faced each other. As she smiled and looked into his eyes, Danny noticed Scott behind her looking very sheepish as he mouthed the word 'sorry'.

'Women, drug dealers and death threats. Really. All you had to do was go on a stag do and get drunk, and you couldn't even do that without killing someone,' Nikki said in an annoyed whisper.

Danny's grin disappeared. He glanced at the vicar looking back at him with a raised eyebrow, then looked at Scott, frowning.

'Don't look at him. He only told me because he thought you were missing, probably dead in a ditch in Spain somewhere,' Nikki said, looking at the vicar as he raised another eyebrow.

'Sorry, love, it wasn't my fault. We were set up and things just got a bit out of hand. Do you still, er, want to get married?' he said, unsure of the answer.

'Of course I want to marry you, you big idiot. Just never try to hide anything from me again.'

'Yes, love,' Danny said, breathing a sigh of relief before both of them turned to the vicar. 'Sorry, we're ready now.'

The vicar cleared his throat and started the ceremony.

'Do you Daniel Pearson, take Nichola Ann Miller, to have and to hold from this day forward, for better or worse, for richer and poorer, in sickness and in health, to love and to cherish, till death do us part?'

ABOUT THE AUTHOR

Stephen Taylor is a successful British Thriller writer. His Amazon bestselling Danny Pearson series has sold well over 200,000 copies, and delighted lovers of the action and adventure thriller genre. Before becoming a novelist, he ran his own business, installing audio visual equipment for homes and businesses.

With the big 50 approaching, Stephen wrote the book he'd always wanted to. That book was Execution Of Faith. A supercharged, action packed roller coaster of a ride that doesn't take itself too seriously. People loved the book so much he wrote a prequel Vodka Over London Ice. Because of the timeline, this became the first in the Danny Pearson Thriller Series.

Born out of his love of action thriller books, Lee Child's Jack Reacher, Vince Flynn's Mitch Rapp and Tom Wood's Victor. Not to mention his love of action movies, Die Hard, Daniel Craig's Bond and Guy Richie's Lock Stock or Snatch. The Danny Pearson series moves along with hard and fast action, no filler, and a healthy dose of humour to move it along.

www.ingramcontent.com/pod-product-compliance
Ingram Content Group UK Ltd.
Pitfield, Milton Keynes, MK11 3LW, UK
UKHW022308020125
3930UKWH00050B/785